MW01114067

# NIMA'S

# NIGHTS

## Erotic Shorts By

# Nima

# NIMA'S NIGHTS

Printed in the United States of America

**ISBN-13:978-0692452035**
**ISBN-10:0692452036**

Printed by Createspace 2015
Published by BlaqRayn Publishing Plus 2015

# Dedication

Taking the time first to thank THE MOST HIGH
for the blessings he has given me...

My family that continues to support my dreams
regardless of the direction in which they
travel...

To my friends and supporters from my writings
to my paintings...thanks for taking this ride...

My BRPP family...It only gets better...
You All Rock!

One Pen...
One Love

**Nima**

# Disclaimer:

*Please be advised this book contains harsh graphic language and story line. It contains violence and may not be suitable for all audiences. It is based strictly on fictitious characters and the creativity of my imagination.*

**"I dare not attempt to be more than they expect for in their eyes I am only mortal. Therefore, in return, not to be more than they expect me to be and attempt my hands at immortality..."**

**Nima Shiningstar-El**

# NIMA'S

# NIGHTS

## Erotic Shorts By

# Nima

# Ripe & Racy Readings

# ZEEK

The cold harsh wind tore through her coat like thousands of small needles piercing the first layer of her skin. Work was hell today from nurses calling out due to flu like symptoms and doctors over medicating themselves due to stress and other work related issues. Tanya had long grown tired of the everyday politics and long hours of the grind. For the past two years, she could feel herself pulling away from the hospital more each day. She had even had words with a nurse that suggested that she get rid of her braids to fit in a little better. It was two weeks ago when Tanya had been running a little late and had not had time to tie her braids up before she walked on the floor. Her braids were long black and reddish. Her eyebrows were arched in a perfect triangle shape and her makeup blended into her dark brown skin perfectly. The way her hair hung when she walked on the floor to her station gave her a sexy sinister look.

"Maybe you should cut your braids off and get a straight weave like the rest of the girls on this floor then you would blend in a little better instead of being so different."

"What the hell are you talking about?" Tanya wasn't in the mood for any mess today.

"I didn't mean it like that." The other nurse was quick to back off.

"First off, 1 love being different and my braids are a part of my culture. Why would I want to look like everyone else? I think you should walk away before you regret it and don't think for one minute that your little remark about everyone else slipped past me because I know exactly what you meant..." Tanya had simply had enough "...I'm so done with this place!"

Her money had been sitting in savings for some time and she did own her own home with no children, a car paid for; she really had no need to stay at the hospital if she truly wanted to leave. Why should she put her dreams on hold? What was holding her back from her dreams? She had always wanted to open a coffee shop. She wanted something small and quaint, a throw back shop, without Wi-fi and going green,without the hustle and bother of modem day technology. She thought of different types of teas and coffees; she could make it work if she focused.

She imagined it so often, she could sometimes taste the Hazelnut coffee or smell the Irish cream.

The tea would be her big seller. She would have green, orange, black, decaf, diet, cherry, half and half. She would call it the T Spot. Sounds like G. Spot because one sip of her goodness and you were hooked. Her special blends would send you into another world. She loved the idea of people being able to unplug from the world and slow it down a bit; to sit and actually have a conversation with the person across the table from you. To take away the mega bites, the fast forward, backspace, delete, likes, etc. made her wet with excitement. To sit engaging in some type of stimulating conversation between two consenting adults or maybe even a group of people was mind blowing in this new age. This would attract early risers as well as late bloomers.

The dream was so real to her, she decided she would make this her last two weeks and put everything into motion. She would give 100 percent of herself to make this happen. For now, she just wanted to get home and soak in the tub and wash the day away.

On the ride home, she thought of the break up with Zeek and how she wanted to call him and invite him over. She missed the sex. Her body needed him now more than ever. He had a way of teasing her and satisfying her all at the same time. She wanted him inside of her, fucking away the stress and drama of the day. She could eat chocolate, have a sip of wine, go to the gym or read her favorite *NIMA* novel yet nothing came close to the pure raw energy of this man. Sometimes it seemed as if he were not real.   She could recall many nights when she would be exhausted and somehow he would breath life into her. She felt dizzy and happy all at the same time.

*************

As soon as Tanya arrived at her German-town home, she turned her music on and headed straight upstairs. Her dog Max met her at the top. Max was an all black German Sheppard. She'd him for two years now and he was well trained. He didn't allow her to make any moves alone once she came in. He was a gift from Zeek.

Loving the single life, she didn't have to bother with the ins and outs of the bullshit that being in a relationship could bring. She also realized that people only wanted you when they could not have you and once they got you, it was the shelf life after that. Her heart had been broken enough and now she was fine.

She did think of Zeek from time to time. Nevertheless, when she wanted him she just closed her eyes and dreamed about him. In her dreams, he was perfect.

The bathroom was black and white with splashes of red. She ran the water filling the tub with milk and honey bath gel. She lit some vanilla candles and walked into her bedroom. Everything called to her. Her bed, her pillows, extra fluffed would make for some wonderful sleep when the time came. She walked to her dresser to find her pleasure box. She took out her vibrator, her motion lotion, some anal beads, and a warm bottle of Moscoto that she kept in her drawer next to her Victoria Secret Reds. Someone told her that if she kept the bottle warm it would go to her head quicker and that's what she wanted. Her lights dim low she felt sexy. She was tired of worrying about what a man thought or whom he was with. She was about to have a date with herself.

Once in the tub, she slid down as far as she could while the muscles from her stomach tightened up from the extremely hot water. This was her time. Washing the day away never felt better. Her yawning was uncontrollable and her eyelids now heavy began to close. It only took a few seconds and she was asleep. Her dreams took her straight to him. Zeek, now kneeling on the side of the tub, slowly unzipped his pants to see if she really wanted it. She wanted it and she didn't hesitate to show him just how bad.

"Are you sure you want this?" He whispered in her dream sensitive ears.

"I'm sure baby..." Her nectar now pooled to lubricate her walls in hot anticipation.

Without any concern or a second thought, he was now one foot in the tub and standing over her head, the perfect positioning for her to get her lips around his massive dick. She always appreciated how it filled her entire mouth with ease but not to the point of dragging across her teeth. He grew as he slid slowly in and out. Now sitting up in the water, she placed her hand around the buckle of his belt to get more control over his movements.

She pulled him in as close as she could get. He loved the way she spit on him every time he pulled all the way out. He couldn't contain himself any longer, so he rushed in undressing and was all over her. They kissed passionately and with his fingers now submerged in the water, he found her opening with ease. She let out a sigh as he opened her and glided back and forth at a steady pace, starting only phase one of their session.

Though they were no longer a couple, some things would never change and that's how well he knew her body. He knew that she was about to cum before she did. He always seemed to show up when she thought of him the most. It was sometimes scary. He never talked about his parents or his up bringing. That's one of the things she didn't like about him; that he always seemed so secretive. Whenever they went out it would never be with people she knew but always friends that he had already. This would make any other female happy but Tanya was tired of it. Yet here he is taking full control of her again or so she thought. She was so engulfed in this dream that she was splashing water on her carpet from all of the movements.

Stepping out of the water in all his beautiful, brown skin dripping wet and smooth as churned caramel, he reached for her hand and led the way to her bedroom. She followed him to the room as if she had no clue where it was.   His 6 foot 2, 210 lbs of sheer soaking pleasure glistened in the dark as if he was glowing. There was an energy in the room that gave her a cold chill down her spine. She ignored it and continued to the bed.

"Zeek, we can't keep doing this. We're not together and I'm confused. Let's not go any further... Zeek, are you listening to me?" He acted as if she wasn't there. Though it was as real as life itself, Tanya was fast asleep in the tub.

Once to the foot of the bed, he shoved her face down ass up and began sucking her clit from the back, allowing his saliva to mix with her juices to flow freely. Never did she notice the man sitting in the chair watching the entire time. He walked towards the bed slowly, leaning over to whisper in her ear.

"You're dead."

With that, he opened his mouth and bit into her neck as Zeek dug his fangs into the other side! As each man bit further into her flesh, Zeek began to cum over and over as if he couldn't stop and with each stroke the life from Tanya's body slowly slipped away...

\* \* \* \* \* \* \* \* \* \* \* \*

As the coroners carried the body from the German-town home, the neighbors gathered around saddened.

"What happened to Tanya?" It was the six million

dollar question.

"They said they found her in a tub full of blood. She must have slit her wrists."

"Suicide?" One neighbor asked. That didn't sound like Tanya at all.

"Damn she seemed so happy and talented. She was such a pretty girl. Just goes to show you never know what someone is going through. Just count your blessing and stay close to GOD."

As the truck pulled away from the crime scene and yellow tape, it took an unexpected tum.

Mrs. Weathers noticed and remarked...

"Why are they going that way? The medical examiner's office is the other way. Nothing is up that hill but the cemetery."

"Well I guess they will figure that out once they come to the dead in..." Mr. Weathers responded to his nosy wife.

The truck slowly pulled to a stop and a gate opened. Once through the gate, Zeek removed his hat and glasses.

"Help me get her inside...we have 30 minutes before she will be awake, uncontrollable and ready to feed..."

# Something About His Eyes

From the time she ran across his photo on the internet, she was intrigued. His comments and beliefs on topics such as religion and politics were so interesting to her, not because of what he said but how he said it and the fact that he was so young to be this well versed. She had always considered herself a smart woman but when it came to him, she felt like a child just opening her eyes to the world around her.

For the most part, all she wanted to do was listen to his voice. She especially loved his take on the world of hip-hop. He had traveled and produced with some of hip-hops royalty. Though he claimed to be from Philly, she could sense a strong accent from another place. It sounded as if it could have been New York easily but she could not be sure.

"You should meet me somewhere tomorrow so we can exchange ideas." He made this statement in such a matter-of-fact way, she was taken aback for a moment.

"Why would we need to do that?" She asked with just a hint of cautious anticipation in her voice.

"I guess I'm just trying to find an excuse to meet you in person."

She had hoped he would say that since she had been feeling this way for some time now.

"Well.." she began very carefully, thinking one step at a time and willing her heart to slow its pace "...today is Monday.. how about Wednesday?"

"How about tomorrow?" He was very persistent.

Nancy was excited yet nervous at the same time.

"Hello?"

His voice had her in that zone.

"Oh...I'm sorry...tomorrow is fine. We...we could meet at the little coffee shop around the corner you said you visited often.. if that's alright with you?"

How she managed to keep her voice from betraying her was a mystery to Nancy.

"Perfect! I will see you tomorrow then." He sounded just as awestruck as she was feeling.

"Yes, see you then..."

Hanging up the phone, she thought of what she would possibly to say to him; deciding what to wear was an entirely different story.

\*\*\*\*\*\*\*\*\*\*\*\*

Waiting for Andre at the coffee shop the next morning, Nancy was a nervous wreck. Maybe he was going to do a no show or...maybe he was already there, watching her from a distance. She suddenly felt jittery, not able to keep still so she pulled out a book and began to read. Knowing that attempting to concentrate on this book was not a real option, she pulled out her cell phone and began to text. She could feel the chair on the other side of her table move so she knew he had just took a seat. She looked up and there he was!

He was sexy as hell! His hands were manly hands. They were the perfect size for gripping her thick frame. His nails were short but clean and well kept. His fingers were a little long but in a erotic way. She could feel them inside of her as they sat across from one another. Those lips damn! They were the perfect shade between dark pink and medium brown. You can tell that this man did not smoke and if he did, it was long ago. He was the perfect height for a sistah to have to stand on her tiptoes to tongue kiss that mouth of his. If only he could see her pussy smiling at him right now. The eye contact made Nancy crazy! He had bedroom eyes. The kind that said

"I want to make love to you while I'm fucking you all crazy..."

As each word came from his lips, she became more and more mesmerized. He talked about this thing he called a no judgment zone and what she concluded from this was that all is fair in the bedroom.

"So what do you say we pick this conversation up tomorrow?" He looked her straight in the eye, smiling that I wanna fuck you smile.

Before she could get a word out he said "great... tomorrow... here... same time."

"Wait! I never said yes."

"Like I said, I will see you here..tomorrow."

He had a lot of nerve but the way he looked at her told the whole story.

****************

Once home, she could think of nothing but seeing him tomorrow. It gave her chills. How with just a few words and gentlemanly gestures he had made her feel so sexy plus he had the brains to match his voice and all his manliness. She wanted him; she also knew he could feel the energy.

The next day, same time.. same spot; the only difference being Andre didn't show up. ***How dare he*** *stand me up! I do not care how sexy and smart he is, I don't play that shit! I'm done!*

When Nancy arrived to work, there was a beautiful arrangement of flowers waiting for her and the card read..

***"Peace, sorry I had to cancel our date but something pressing came up at the last minute and though I should have reached out to you, it totally escaped my mind. I hope this does not put me in a bad light with you. Let's build tomorrow if possible. Get at me..."***

She loved the gesture but for some reason she loved the note even more. She thought to herself as she read the card for the third time. ***Ok.. if Mr. Let's build wants a run for his money I will give him one...***

As night slowly turned into day and she drifted into sleep, she could hear his voice and feel his hands all over her. She could smell him and her mouth opened as if she was making love, attempting to catch her breath. She bit her bottom lip and softly talked to a ghost. She asked him to make love to her and call her bitches, something she would've slapped the shit out of someone for even thinking. But, tonight she was in his no judgment zone. She commanded him to go deeper and she pinched her nipples to increase the pleasure. She moved her ass to his invisible groove...

***********

The phone broke through her dream with a vengeance just before climax and she was not happy at all.

"Hello!" She screamed angrily into the speaker.

"Did I call at a bad time?"

It took a few seconds to realize who was on the other end.

"No, it's not a bad time but why are you calling me this late?" She was still rather testy.

"I was thinking about you and well... I couldn't sleep. Tell me...what are you wearing?"

"Hello?" He was afraid he had freaked her out.

The phone was silence for at least five seconds before she spoke again.

"I'm here... I'm   wearing a black tee shirt, if you must know." She had already begun to tingle with excitement but she wasn't gonna let **him** know that.

"Take it off." His demand was soft yet firm.

"What?"

"Take it off,   put the phone on speaker and open your legs."

She was doing exactly what she was told. This was something she'd been wanting for years! For a man to take control of her in every way possible without that thugged out bullshit.

"Are your legs open?" His voice was low, husky, caressing her like intense feathers on her sensitive flesh.

"Yes."

"Tell me you want me." Silence

"I said tell me you want me!" The longer it took her to answer, the louder he became and it sent vibrations to all of her lower levels.

"Tell me you want me to fuck you." There was now urgency in his demand.

"I want you to fuck me." It came out in a breathless moan.

"Tell me you want me down your throat."

She told him and meant every word.

"Open your mouth..."

And just as in the dream, just before he called, she did just that.

With each word he whispered, she pleasured herself. Her fingers met her opening and the moistness that met her tips was truly undeniable. She had been so confined and restricted in past relationships that she was elated and elevated by the new possibilities. By the end of the phone conversation or lack thereof, she was out of breath and wanting all of him right then.

Walking around the office the next day and keeping a poker face was hard. She giggled to herself as she reminisced on the previous night's events. She didn't realize how obvious it was until her coworker came over laughing and saying..

"Someone had a good time last night. You got this entire office lit and glowing off love."

For the next two weeks, the same time each night, she sat by the phone waiting for and like clockwork, he called. Every night they laughed, talked and had the most amazing phone sex ever! She often wondered if she was one of many on the list to get a call from him at night but she was so gone that she didn't even care.

One night it happened. She told him that she needed to say something to him; however, she wasn't sure how he would take it. She took a deep breath, closed her eyes and told him she loved him. *What the hell am I doing* she thought    She covered her mouth as if it was a mistake, wishing she could take it back.

"I love you back..." *Wait what did he just say!*

The phone went silent for a few seconds before they said goodnight.

\*\*\*\*\*\*\*\*\*\*\*

She was so happy to have the next day off to collect her thoughts. Her bed was her sanctuary and her remote was her faithful partner. She channel surfed for the most part of the morning until she decided to take a shower and freshen up.    The night before had her floating. She was still in shock about her confession and even more so because of Andre's confession to her. Was this some type of game he was playing because she'd had her share of the BS! She was fine with what they had going on without him playing with her heart. And she never believed in saying something that she didn't mean. She needed to think some things through before she spoke to him again.

As she did each Friday night, she called up her favorite take out place and ordered. This would definitely be a self-date night with vibrator and lotions on deck. The delivery person was taking longer than usual so she was not giving a nice tip.

"Finally, damn it took you long enough..." and without asking any further questions opened the door to Andre!

"What are you doing here?" She asked, a bit flustered.

"Is there a problem with me stopping past to check on you?" He wondered *why the attitude?*

"No, but where did you come from?"

"How did you even know *I* was home or that *I* didn't have company?"

"I saw your car and took a chance...Oh, by the way, I have your food. *I* paid for it so now you owe me." He winked as he stepped into her living room, closing the door and the world out behind him.

"What do I owe you..."

As music played and candles burned throughout the day into the late night, Andre and Nancy made love, had sex, fucked, and created new universes. From the front door to the steps, over the arm rest of the sofa, against the wall, in the shower and every place in the house. Their scent was alluring and intoxicating. As she once again pulled up from his throbbing love, she could feel every vein. She loved the texture of him.

When she came up for air the 3rd time, he grabbed her face, kissing her deeply.

"I love you and don't forget it ever."

She couldn't understand the electric and energy between them but she loved all of it.

# The Demon on the Bus

Sitting, cloud watching
The sun a super sexy orange as it slowly
begins its transition Thinking..
(Thank You GOD for your love and
moments like this.)
Jealous as He is real wants His place in
my thoughts as well
A sexy, sensual, erotic smell invaded my senses
Curiosity I tried to ignore
The smell invaded more and more
As in a movie scene slowly
turning in the smells direction.. I
knew I had to pray for protection
He had to be demonic to be that fine
It had to be a crime...


Someone is getting hurt tonight
Chaos will follow him tonight
Trying to look away
My eyes would not stray
I fixed on his face unaware of time and place
Skin so smooth and perfect light caramel
Tall enough to have to stand on my toes to reach his
lips
I told myself get a grip
If he were not a demon then he was created in a lab
Looked so good and yet it hurt so bad
Haircut low and natural
I move further away because my whole body shook

## NIMA'S NIGHTS

I had an uneasy feeling about this man
I just couldn't understand
I wanted him off my bus

Getting out of my sight was necessary
I said a silent prayer and opened my eyes
He got off the bus and we slowly drove by
My face to the window one more look at this guy
He gave me a smile and then winked his eye...

# Inbox Odyssey

The rain fell in a perfect rhythm against her window. She thought to herself how sexy the slight breeze was against her velvet skin. Just another quiet night in her small apartment. She had grown somewhat tired and bored with the usual small talk that she had encountered in her travels of this fish-town area of Philadelphia. Now standing on her balcony, she opens up all of the buttons of her shirt to expose her nipples to the cool night air. She was happy that he had left some of his clothing behind when they parted ways. She walked towards her computer that sat on her bed and giggled as she reminisced on a few days ago when she accidentally inboxed a total stranger thinking it was her best friend Brenda.

She had told Brenda just the other day how bored she was with most men in the area and though it was fast becoming a flourishing, colorful place with all its new clubs and restaurants, she still found no one to stimulate her intellect and her body at the same time. She was happy that her former lover Mr. Tuesday night better known as Steven decided he wasn't ready for a serious relationship and packed up some of his things while she was at work.

Steven did know how to fuck though. His lips and dick were perfect in every way possible. He was a passionate kisser. He started by small light kisses from her nose down to her lips before pushing his way full into her mouth. One kiss would have your panties on the floor. That being said he was a horrible finisher. He went strong for about 20 minutes and would be done for the rest of the night. That left her in bed smoking a cigar and playing with her pussy trying not to wake him.

When Catherine told Brenda this story for the first time, she laughed so hard she almost chocked on a piece of candy but once this became a regular phone call she told Catherine about this website she frequents. Catherine now sat on the bed wishing she had the courage to call her ex...Charles. Charles knew her like a book and read her on a regular basis. He loved to watch her throw little fits of jealousy and try to withhold pussy because she had an attitude. She met Charles at the law library one day. By the next week, they were having dinner and holding hands as they walked through the park.

She could feel her pulse starting to race just thinking about Charles..But that was the past. She chose her career over him and that was that. Now lying across the bed, she caressed the keys, contemplating inboxing this total stranger that caught her attention for a split second.

"What the hell.. It's not like we are video chatting.. its only an inbox." Clicking on his name she decided to keep it simple...

@SometimesSingle-Hey I know this sounds crazy but I thought about you today. I know you may not remember but I accidentally sent you a message the other day. I love your profile but I have been warned to stay away from people with no picture. Anyway just giving you a shout out. Have a great night.

Catherine went to tum off her computer when she heard that little ring sound that told you that someone was responding to your instant message.

@Katnip-Hey you..I remember and how are we today? Honestly I have been thinking of you also. Yes crazy I know but it is what it is. What are you doing

@Sometimes single-I was actually about to throw in a movie and just lay across my bed. I'm off for the next two days so I figured I should spend at least one of those days in bed.

@Katnip-I totally understand that. I work long hours and really like to relax when I can. So I guess I should ask you what type of things do you like to get into when possible?

@Sometimes Single-I love movies and reading books. I do go dancing from time to time but my passion would really be to get on a plane and go somewhere. What about you?

@Katnip-It depends on the woman that I am with at the time. I love romantic walks and watching the stars but I love to watch a woman pleasure herself.

Catherine sat looking at the screen until the words "hello" came across.

@Katnip-Are you still there? I didn't mean to be too forward but that's just the way I am. I don't mean any harm by it.

@Sometimes Single-No it's fine...I was getting comfortable. You can speak as freely as you like. I am a grown ass woman.

He knew by her response that he could take this to a entirely different level. He thought to himself..let the games begin!

@Katnip-So grown ass woman, what do you look like because your profile is filled with tropical fish.

@Sometimes Single-Does it really matter all you need to know is that I am a woman and I work hard.

@Katnip-What are you wearing right now and don't lie.

@Sometimes Single-Red thongs and red heels.

He knew she was telling a lie but he played along anyway

@Katnip-I wish I could see you. Why don't you click that face time button and let's see where it takes us

She thought for a moment and was a little nervous but it's over the computer.. what harm could it do but be put on YouTube or something. She went to her dresser and pushed her toys to the side to retrieve a black and purple mask that she had worn for a Halloween party one year. No one would recognize her. Maybe she should grab the wig and really perform. Fuck it!

@Sometimes Single-I don't mind if you don't.

When they clicked their computers to the app, both were pleasantly surprised to see the other person. To her astonishment, he too wore a mask but there was something very familiar about him.

@Katnip-You are beautiful.

@Sometimes Single-You look good as well. I'm glad we decided to do this. I don't really get into stuff like this but you made me feel comfortable.

They talked for hours laughing and joking all in the nude. It felt so natural. This turned into a twice a week thing until they decided to take it to the next level.

@Katnip-I want to watch you play with your pussy

tonight. I need to see you cum all over those pretty little fingers of yours and then put them in your mouth and lick it off.

She was ready to do whatever he asked and then some. Outside her window she could see flashing lights from a fire truck go by but what she didn't expect to see was the same light flashing behind his window on the screen. She tried to put it out of her mind until she heard the neighbor's dog barking yet she could also hear it coming from the screen. She was now convinced that he lived in her building and she may even know him.

@Sometimes Single-Don't you think its time we exchange real names?

@Katnip-You're right. My name is Greg.

@Sometimes Single-My name is Catherine

@Katnip-That feels better already. Now when you slide those fingers inside, you can call out my name. Let me see that beautiful pussy of yours.

She was so nervous and excited at the same time, she had to remember to breathe. Following his every instruction to the letter, she was being controlled by a stranger and wanted more. Over time, they had a love affair completely over the computer and nothing was off limits. Sometimes candles were lit and soft music played like Barry White's "Practice What You Preach".

@Katherine-Could you give me a minute Greg, I need to use the bathroom.

@Greg-Sure, whatever you need to do to have that pretty ass ready. I will just listen to Barry until you bring that sexy ass back to me.

Catherine was up and on her tiptoes so he couldn't hear how far she was going but she could hear the music coming from inside her building. She put on a bathrobe and opened her door. She thought for a minute how crazy this was and not to mention, dangerous. She followed the sound three doors down and took a listen just to be certain. Sure enough, she could hear Greg's voice coming from the apartment singing to the very same Barry White song they were about to have some fun with. She took a deep breath... knocking on the door.

Once the door opened,

"Hello Greg..." For a few seconds, he just stood starring at her.

"Damn, how did you, I mean... **where** did you come from?"

"Before you say another word, why don't you invite me in?" She almost burst out laughing from the look of total shock on his beautiful face.

"Sure, I'm just trying to figure our how you found me?"

As he talked, she locked the door and walked towards him. Not to be outdone in his own home, he picked her up, leaving her red painted toenails swinging from his arms. He could smell the fragrance of cocoa butter lotion coming from her skin. It smelled delicious. Now laying her down gently on the bed and kissing her so softly. They felt like soft snowflakes landing on her hot flesh.   It was not starting the way she'd thought; it was even better. He touched her face as if he needed to examine her up close. Brushing his fingers across her soft skin made him feel like a man. He told her stories about beautiful places beyond this planet. He described each place to paint a perfect picture.    It was as if she had been to these very places and bathed in their beauty.

That night Catherine made love for the first time. It was not just sex or fucking. It was not just masturbating and squirting. It was emotional, spiritual, and beyond anything this world had ever offered her before.    She felt as if she were being lifted from the bed and she had faith in every movement.

# Dinner Date

Summer in Philly was always off the hook; that is, a summer where any and everything could happen. But the summer of 2000 was something totally different. For starters, most of my girlfriends were pissed and angry because they had maxed out their credit cards thinking that the world was ending. That Y2K thing. Once the clock struck midnight, listen, anything was possible but I am a firm believer that only GOD knows the time.

Anyway, people were draining their bank accounts, fighting and anything they wanted to do before someone turns the lights out on us. It was also the summer that I was introduced to a threesome and watching orgies among other things but we will talk about that later.

**Oscar...**

Oscar was something different. I remember the first time I introduced him to my small circle. My girlfriend Ava was having a dinner party at her house. Ava, Maggie and I decided we should bring dates. At the time, I had just moved into my new apartment building and had not met one person. I met Oscar on the elevator. I pushed the button for the 9th floor and he pushed the button for the Penthouse. The top floor must be nice.

"Well that's where my boss lives. I check in with him every morning before I go to the office." He had a very nice smile.

"Oh. Well, that must keep you busy?" I responded with a shoulder shrug.

"So how do you like living in the building Ms.." he waited for my response as I finally got a clue and said..

"Nicole. My name is Nicole...and you are?" There was that smile again.

"Oscar. I'm Oscar Ramirez." Oscar Ramirez had a nice voice as well.

"Well Oscar Ramirez this is my floor. It was nice talking to you..."

This little exchange went on for 2 weeks. Then one day Oscar gets on just as the elevator door is about to close. He was carrying a bouquet of the most gorgeous flowers.

"Oh wow, those are beautiful flowers.. she is very lucky."

That nice smile was there yet this time it was extra playful.

"What makes you say she?"

"I mean if there is a he that's cool too. I do not judge." But thinking of all this man going to waste with another dude kinda bothered me.

"Well, what if I told you they were for you... what would you say?"

I looked him dead in his thick glasses, nerd suit and corn ball hair cut and twisted my lips.

"Why would they be for me?" Why indeed!

"I think you are pretty when I saw these, I thought of you." That alluring smile again. It was awesome despite the glasses.

I was stuck on stupid but I thanked him anyway. I thought for a second *maybe I should invite him to dinner, he looks harmless enough. I know where he works and besides, if he tried something, I would just stomp his short ass with my boots.*

"Hey listen, my girlfriend's having a dinner party at her house up Mount Airy. Would you like to come?" The smile turned to a full out grin.

"Are you sure?" A bit of a frown wrinkled his forehead, but never reached his eyes or that smile.

"Why not. It will be fun... drinks, music, dinner, nice people."

His head did this funny snap thing and I swear I actually saw him mentally make the decision to accept my invite.

"Alright, as long as you are sure its OK."   He was so excited, I couldn't resist.

"It's only dinner... we're not getting engaged." It didn't move him one bit.

"True..." he chuckled and it was actually kinda sexy.

"..well what time should I pick you up?"

"How about we meet downstairs in front of the building?" He nodded his agreement.

"Well until then Mr. Ramirez and thanks for the flowers."

For the rest of the day, she wondered what made him give her the flowers.   She never liked short men but there was something kind of weird and cute about him. She could not even imagine telling her friends she was bringing an Hispanic dinner date. She tried not to look at it as a date but it was what it was. *Hell a date is a date* she thought.

Nicole took a much needed shower and laid across her bed for a quick nap. When she woke, feeling refreshed, she pulled out a little Red form fitting dress she'd had in closet for about two years, waiting for it to fit just right. It had been a combination of drinking plenty of water, exercise and tossing the junk food that put her figure in the perfect position to compliment the dress. It had been her inspiration, her motivation and now she was wasting all her sexiness on some pencil pushing, walking pocket protector.

At dinner that night, she found herself extremely taken in by Oscar. Even her three girlfriends Maggie, Jackie, and Trina, along with their dates, seem to hang on his every word. It was as if he had a gift for words. He told jokes, talked politics and religion; however, he talked mostly about the sexual revolution and the beauty of a woman's sensual body. I looked around the table and saw the men nodding like men in the barbershop on Saturday and the women waiting for his next word. Everyone seemed to be in a trance including me.

He wanted to give an example of his theory, including me in his little demonstration as a test subject. I must admit I was uncomfortable with the idea but my girlfriends encouraged me. When I first stood up, I felt silly but once he began to touch me, I could feel my nipples becoming erect. I felt my skin come alive. My friends took notice as well;

they began to blush and look away but the men kept their eyes on me without breaking a glance.

Suddenly without warning, Oscar spoke in a gentle yet commanding tone...

"Maggie, come up and feel how warm Nicole's skin is since I've touched her like that."

Mags was having none of that!

"No I'm cool." She announced, vigorously shaking her head,

"Maggie, Nicole is your friend... she's not a stranger come on.    This is one of the things I have been sharing and demonstrating to people. We are so detached from being who we really want to be that we are afraid of our own shadows and as soon as someone questions that or opens a door to another way of thinking then that person is labeled some type of pervert or crazy."

Maggie looked at the others seated around the table and when she got no opposition, she came up. Oscar placed Maggie's fingertips on my nipples and I almost fainted. I felt extremely excited. Oscar talked in my ear like a coach on game day but really soft and sexy. I could not figure out what was going on.

One bye one, he invited all three women and all three men up to take part in this demonstration of sexual behavior with me as his test subject. Maggie made small circles on my left nipple. Her mouth was warm and inviting. She licked so softly. Her tongue was like three thick rose petals put together dipped in some warm solution. Jackie had my dress up, gently kissing my plump ass. My head dipped back and though I attempted to control myself, I was losing the battle. Trina had my panties in her hands, as my pussy became her canvass and her mouth the paintbrush. I felt every lick and suck she made. My body was in a state of eruption and at any minute, I would explode. I wanted to fall to the floor but Oscar and the three men who were talking to me as I was being manipulated they held me up.

My entire body was on fire; I could feel my legs trembling. That's when the men carried me to the dinner table. Everything was immediately pushed to the floor and I was laid on my back like the main course. I looked over in the direction of the crash to see Maggie and Trina in a scissor position grinding one another. The sounds of pleasure from the women turned everyone on in the room. Oscar now had Jackie on all fours and his tongue was in her ass. He was so far inside, you almost lost sight of his entire face. To watch her ass wiggle and bounce to allow him further entrance made my clit throb.

My body was now being pulled towards the edge of the table. Fingers probed my inner walls while a wet mouth massaged saliva into my nipples. White flesh entered my mouth as Jackie's date stood over my head dipping every bit of him down my throat. Never had I experienced such pleasure and excitement all at once. Slurping and sucking sounds followed by moans created a highly intense atmosphere and I was in the middle of it all. I felt possessed; I could not get enough. I titled my head in Oscar's direction and I could see him stroking his dick as he watched me being feasted upon.

Now for the third time tonight, I was having an orgasm. Only this time I could see Oscar at the same instance, spilling his juices all over the carpet. Slowly slipping into a state of Utopia, all I could think at that very moment was...

*Who in the world was Oscar and where did he come from all of a sudden ?*

# Sharing Everything

The sun massages her dark brown skin as she sits on her patio. The gentle wind blows away the troubles of the day. As Tee sits and sips her perfectly blended cup of mocha..she can't help but think of the chaos that helped her to arrive at this very peaceful place. Who would have known that she, a perfectly rational woman, could and would make such irrational decisions? To think just the night before she had completely and without reservation given herself to him.

She thought of the moment it had happened. His voice was as smooth as silk and his approach as radiant as the stars. She had never before seen a star so bright which made it easy for her to become captivated by its beauty. He'd come to her the first night somewhat apprehensively, afraid to venture through uncharted territory. He thought to himself, took a deep breath and asked her to dance. In time she would find this to be an act well perfected.

"I can't believe that I finally got the nerve to ask you to dance Ms. Lady."

Tee looked into the eyes of the sexy stranger and

in her soft, innocent voice replied

"What were you waiting for"?

To his surprise she had stopped dancing and waited for him to respond.

"By the way I'm Victor". Sexy with a nice voice....not bad!

"Nice to meet you Victor and I'm Tee."

"So what is Tee short for?"

"It's short for Tina." She was getting lost in those eyes, but he was messing up the vibe by asking so many questions.

"Tina is such a beautiful name, why would you shorten it?"

"It's a long, rather boring story." One excuse is as good as another.

"Well, if you allow me to take you for a cup of coffee tomorrow you can tell me all about it..."

Just the thought of him made her tingle so she could only imagine. She could have this feeling as often as needed. She had long grown tired of the creams, lubricants, beads, and vibrators that lined her closet shelves. Though her devices were the safest form of sex she'd ever had, she needed a man. She needed Victor. She could feel his breath in her face as he opened his mouth to share the nectar from his fingers with her. As she opened her legs for him to get deeper inside...Tina!!!

Tina was so caught up in her dream, she was almost late for work. Had it not been for her roommate coming into her bedroom she would still be dreaming.

"Girl I don't know what you were dreaming about in there last night but that shit must have been good because your ass was making some serious sounds. I think you need a man before you accidentally find yourself trying to tip toe in my room and you know damn well Kenya don't play that."

They shared a laugh but Tina knew she was long overdue. Tina touched her face and then traced a bead of sweat down her neck. How could it have been dream? She could smell the scent of sex in the air and the moisture of passion was evident on her sheets. She had 25 minutes to shower, fix her hair, and grab a cup of mint tea.

"Girl I wish I could have been in your dream." Kenya gave Tee a playful wink.

"What makes you say that?" Tee was suddenly a little protective of her dream lover.

"All I'm saying is he was putting his thing down." Kenya laughed while she gyrated her hips.

"Girl bye. I promise to tell you later. In the meantime, don't forget it's your turn to pay the cable bill."With that, she hit the shower running.

At work, she rushed through her day and even got a heads up on some things that she had planned for tomorrow. She had worked for Mr. Strathmore for a little over a year now. He was very demanding and she prided herself on always staying two steps ahead of him but today was something different. She had an extra pep in her step and Victor on her brain.

Tee watched the clock and realized she had 15 minutes before her coffee date with Victor. To the ladies room she walked with purse in had. She stood in front of the mirror checking for left over food particles in between her teeth. She quickly dumped the contents of her hunter green clutch bag on the sink. Looking for her toothbrush, lipstick, and condoms. She thought for a minute and decided to put the condoms in her bra. There had been a few occasions where the condoms were just out of reach. But that's another story. She was ready. Her heart raced as a child excited to meet Santa Claus for the first time.

As she walked towards the table, her hands began to sweat. She couldn't very well shake hands with him now so she chose to hug him. The embrace put her up against his hard chest. She could smell cool water cologne invading her nostrils.

"Hello again Tee." Yes yes yes!!!

"Hello Victor."

"So I chose a booth in the back if that's OK with you?" *You could choose a booth on the moon and as long as you were in it, it would be just fine with me..*

They talked and laughed as old friends catching up. Victor suddenly looked deeply into Tee's eyes and said...

"I want you to slowly take your panties off and give them to me." She bit her bottom lip which meant I'm feeling horny but what came out of her mouth was...

"I'm not wearing any."

Victor was use to having the upper hand in any situation but he nearly dropped his cup at her response. He quickly collected his thoughts as he put his cup to his lips

"I didn't think you would actually meet me here today." He just sounded so deep and sincere.

"I can't lie... last night I tossed and turned thinking of you."

Victor removed his jacket and moved his body closer to Tee. She attempted to watch his eyes for his next move but he moved too swiftly. She could feel his warm hand moving up her thigh.    He instructed her to open her legs.  As he began to insert his fingers inside her hidden treasure, all she could do was close her eyes and position herself to allow him complete access. Between low moans she could hear him say.. "follow me to the restroom.."

As she followed him to the restroom, she could feel the left over juices dancing down her inner thighs. She thought to herself how crazy and outside the box this was for her. She had    always been so appropriately put together or at least to a degree. The closer she got to the men's room, she could smell the strong scent of urine and cool water cologne mixed.    The lights were dim and she felt nervous but there was not turning back now! She wanted this to happen!

As soon as she walked through the door Victor grabbed her hand, leading her to an empty stall.    She could tell by the way he did it, with such ease and precision, that he'd done this before but it was too late. She had seen this type of thing on the movies but to be living in this moment was an out of body experience for her.

Now kissing her as if his life depended upon it, his muscle grew with each breath. She began to unzip his pants and immediately assumed the position of kneeling over the black toilet. She ripped open the condom she had in her bra and passed it back to Victor. Her legs trembled and before she could take another breath, he had entered her with such unexpected tenderness. Though he was unimaginably blessed and could have easily changed her walk instantly, he took his time and allowed her time to regroup after each stroke. He held her by her waist, tracing beads of sweat up and down her spine. Her weave swung back and forth, as he slowly picked up the pace of his thrusts.

Tee was on such a high. She moaned and hit her hands against the wall of the stall. At times, she had to remember to breathe because she was caught up in the passion and lust of it all. At that moment she could care less if anyone else was in the men's room to hear.

"Tee I have thought about you for so long. I knew you would see things my way and come to me if I just gave you enough time..."

She never gave a second thought to what he had just said. All she could do was accommodate his movement by pushing her body back and at times holding her weave to keep it from going into the toilet.

Victor began to pick up the pace even more now! He got excited the louder she yelled. Her breath was rapid and she felt herself arriving! He must have felt her body ready to explode because he picked up the pace even faster and was now riding and pounding her pussy as if he was drilling for oil and felt the gush.

"Baby I have been..waiting for..."

Victor couldn't finish another word, he gripped her by both shoulders and started to cum. She wanted to see it for herself so she squatted down in front of him as he let the rest explode onto her lips and chin, .even opening her mouth so she could taste what he now called her juice.

"Come here." He demanded softly.

With shaken legs, she was helped to her feet so Victor could lick and share the passion nectar in her mouth.

"Tee, are you alright."

Victor asked, out of breath himself and waiting for her to reply.

"I'm fine.. just confused."

"I don't want to ruin this so maybe you could call me tonight and that way I can have a chance to think some things through."

Now Victor was a bit baffled.

"Umm well, OK but I will be in a little late since I have some things to attend to but as soon as I get in I will call you." Tee's legs were still trembly and she knew walking straight would take a minute.

"That's fine. I a need minute to get myself together as best as I can before I walk out of here. I need a bath and a nap."

She walked to the sink with Victor directly behind her. A look of bewilderment covered her face.

"What? You didn't actually think I was leaving you in the men's bathroom alone did you?" He chuckled a bit as he shook his head in the negative.

He pulled some paper towels from the dispenser, adding soap from the wall. She never protested or moved as Victor added warm water to the towels and began to slowly caress her throbbing clit. The massage he gave her while cleansing her made her want to open her legs for him to penetrate her once more. His fingers now traced her outer lips and peeled back the layer slowly sliding his finger inside. The way she gripped the sink let him know that she was ready for another pounding. This man had her floating and she was not ready to come back to earth just yet. She felt so free and liberated. Her body and mind felt alive! When she looked into his eyes, she felt trapped and spiritually disconnected from everything in her past. She could see nothing but this man in front of her.

Walking out of the restroom, Tee bumped into an older gray haired man trying to make his way to handle his business. He smiled at the two of them as they passed, causing her to blush. Once outside, the sky seemed a perfect shade of blue. The birds seemed to be singing a happy song and the air smelled sweet. Victor, who now seemed extremely anxious, kept looking at his watch and talking on his phone in riddles to someone. Quickly turning to face her, he kissed Tee on the lips with a closed mouth and rushed away.

Once she got inside of her car, she paused for a moment to think about what had just taken place. She touched her breast and her lips wondering what would become of her and Victor. Since she had moved to Philly, she really had not had time for any serious relationships and she damn sure did not have anybody that could make her body feel the way Victor did. The hairs on her arms stood up and she tingled each time she thought about him and it.

"Hello."

"Girl! I just fucked the shit out of this nigga in the men's room of the restaurant!"

"What the hell are you talking about?" Kenya was not buying it!

"The dude I was telling you about. I met him for coffee and we hit the fuckin bathroom hard girl!"

"Bitch stop lying!" Kenya was beyond shocked!

"I had to call you. I'm on my way in but I couldn't wait that long and, oh my god, his dick nearly split my shit girl but I took it like a boss!" She was laughing like a kid.

"Details when you get in... dinner is on me. You good with Chinese? I told you Philly got the best Chinese?"

"I'm good with Chinese but make sure you get plenty of fortune cookies." Tee was feelings very fortunate.

"Why? You already gave your cookies away?"

"Bye girl."Kenya was still laughing when Tee hung up on her.

On the ride home, Tee had a flashback of Victor telling her that he had been wanting her for some time now though she never met him before the other day.

She had to admit to there was something in his voice and the smell of his cologne that did seem a tad familiar but with all of these fine men walking the streets of Philadelphia, it didn't even make sense to wonder. She would definitely be seeing him as often as possible!

She walked through the door expecting to smell take out.

"Hey girl I don't smell no Chinese food up in here!"

"Something came up so I put your food in the microwave and when you're done, you might want to hang in your room for the rest of the night." Kenya sounded like she might be busy.

"Say no more.. I get the point. I guess I will have to brag another day. I am exhausted anyway; I need to get my ass in the tub..."

Walking to the bathroom, she could not help but smile and think to herself how telling her friend about her episode most likely made her horny and want to call her boo over. She was always talking about her boo. He so fine, he so smart, he smells so good. Every time you turn around, she was buying him another bottle of that Cool Water Cologne... *That's the smell... Cool Water cologne! Every time he comes over I smell that smell!*

Though her mind wandered for a moment, she realized that she had never met him, she could not even remember his name ever being spoken of. He had always been referred to as her boo or her baby.

"Let me stop tripping and get my ass in this tub and to my comer of the world before Mr. Cool Water comes over..."

Tee went into the bathroom and immediately turned on the water. She filled it with her peach mango body bath form Victoria Secrets. She allowed the fragrance to take over. She lit some black love candles, took off her black satin robe and slippers, and slid slowly down into the hot water. As the water covered her body, she could feel her stomach muscles tighten up. The water felt so good between her legs. She allowed herself to relax and slowly drift into a light nod.

Tee awoke to a now slightly cooler tub so she bathed and got out. Putting on her robe and slippers, she could hear her friend in the bedroom moaning and being slapped on the ass. She stayed in the bathroom sitting on the side of the tub giggling at the way the bed banged against the wall and though the music was up somewhat high she could still hear the guy calling her a bitch and telling her to take all of his dick and stop running from it.

As she walked towards her own room, her emotions ran high as she could finally make out the voice of the man in the other room..It was Victor! The man who had earlier sexed her uncontrollably was now in the room with her friend. This is why he had said he waited for this moment for some time now. Had he planned this all along? He must have. She did not know what to do. She was hurt, angry, confused, and pissed. She had to see for herself. She had to make sure, before she did anything.

She slowly opened the door and watched for a few minute as they fucked as if it was the last time they would see one another. She watched as his dick slid in and out with ease and imagined it was her. The way cum dripped over her ass, even the way her ass bounced up and down when he pumped into her. Suddenly Victor looked over at the door and smiles.

"Come join us."

Tee was frozen until her friend turned towards the door, pulled back the sheets, and said

" Come join us."

# The Deacon's Destruction

Thinking back on my childhood I can see where my fascination for a man of GOD came into play. Growing up in my mother's home, you went to church all the time. I did not have any friends outside of church because all of my friends went to church. Every Sunday my family sat in the third pew. Not only did I go to a church but a Baptist   church! Baptist churches had the best food and the best music. After church on Sundays, we would go into another room where there would be long tables of food. Cornbread, Potato salad, baked macaroni & cheese, ham, chicken, collard greens, and all types of cakes and pies. My mamma would stand behind the table with Sister Brown, Sister White, and Sister Smith making those plates and giggling while some of the brothers of the church flirted with them.

The music made you want to get up and dance. You could feel it in your chest and the best singers in Philly took center stage on Sundays. But most of all, we had Deacon Glass. Deacon Glass was the youngest member of the Pastor's board and he was fine.   He was so friendly too but none of us girls cared about that; all we cared about was how sexy he was. All the women loved

Deacon Glass. He was fun and he knew everyone by name. He knew all the latest dances and all the new slang we used in the street. Pastor Glass was Deacon Glass' father, had started this church and was the Pastor until his death three years ago. Knowing that his son was too young to handle such a task, he place Pastor Holmes to lead the flock until his son was ready.

Everyone had a crush on Deacon Glass; especially me. I would sit and watch him stand-up front ready to welcome new members. He had such a beautiful voice.

"Carole, girl do you hear me talking to you?" I had been in such a daydream about the Deacon that I did not here my mother call me to leave.

"Yes mom, I'm coming." I didn't want to leave his presence.

"Your father is waiting outside blocking traffic, waiting for us."

"Mom why doesn't daddy come to church?" I had asked this question many times and each time, I got the same response.

"That's between your father and the Lord." I really did not care. I just wanted to side track my mother so she wouldn't ask me what I was thinking about. I mean really I was only 14 and what else am I going to think about but boys?

It has been seven years since I've stepped foot in a church. Since my parents divorced when I was fourteen, I have been living with my Aunt in New York. Today the only person who was able to get me back in church was my mother. I visited my mother often and we talked on the phone as if we were best friends but for some reason after she and my dad split she was a broken spirit to a degree. We did many things together but whenever she would mention church, I would change the subject. Somehow, I blamed church for my parent's breaking up. I know it sounds crazy but all I remember is my dad never wanting to come inside.

However, today was a special day for my mother, she was receiving some type of recognition from the church so I went. You never know who you are going to meet at church so I made sure to put on one of my tight low cut dresses and my purple pumps to dress it up or down depending on how you looked at it and to finish it off, I put on my purple church hat. *I hope this is not an all day thing because I have things to do when I leave.*

"Oh, I'm so sorry, I didn't see you standing there. I'm trying to get to the ladies room before the ceremony starts..."

"Well let me get out of your way sis. And if I may, I just want to let you know you are one sexy woman." I gave him a real look now and there was something vaguely familiar about this fine church brother.

"Alright now, don't get into any trouble in the house of the Lord." I smiled and so did he briefly...the smile did it.

"Maybe I should and that way I can take it right to the alter and pray about it."

By now, I had forgotten all about the bathroom and was listening to Mr. Smooth. He was fine as hell and then it hit me *I'm standing directly in front of Deacon Glass*. He did not realize who I was. He was still fine as ever and his breath smelled like peppermint. Damn I remember dreaming about him and all the things I could not do because I was too young. Wow how time changes things. *Right now I want to push this man up against the wall and suck his dick*. I figured I'd have a little fun before I went to the bathroom.

"So how about you stop talking and start doing."

At that point, he began to stutter a little. I could see that he was just talking shit and he needed some encouragement.

"How about you follow me to the bathroom?" He

never said a word but he followed just the same. When he walks out of this bathroom, he would definitely be coming back and I am going to make damn sure of that.

Once in the bathroom I said..

"I do not want you to get into any trouble so just watch..."

I pulled my dress up to reveal my black and purple lace Victoria Secret panty and bra set I'd just purchased; immediately he started to pray. I opened a stall door and sat on one of the toilets. I opened my legs and pulled my panties to the side. He was rubbing his dick through he suit pants. My left hand held my pussy open while two fingers on my right hand glided in and out until I started to glisten. He came over to me, massaging his manhood until it oozed. He never penetrated me, he just rubbed the head of his dick against me and let it all run down the outside of my pussy and I was happy with that for now.

We did not say a word afterward, he just stood against the stall holding his now limp dick while I took some of what he left behind and put it to his lips. I stood at the sink and watched him in the mirror as he walked out.

"Shit, let me hurry up and get out of this bathroom and back to this ceremony..."

As things got underway, I took a seat in the back of

the church so I would not distract the deacon. I watched as everything took place and the Deacon gave my mother, Sister Tammy Tate, her plaque. Everyone stood on their feet and stayed their while the choir sang and The Pastor Prayed. I was so proud of my mother. Now it was time for the board to do their thing with greeting and shaking hands. My mother could not wait to get me up to the front of the church and reintroduce me to everyone.

"Deacon Glass, my baby made it all the way from New York. Remember Carole? She was fourteen last time you saw her.. now she is a hard working Fashion Production Specialist..".

The look on his face was sheer fear. It was as if he'd seen a ghost. He did not say a word until I reached out my hand and said.

I remember.. Deacon Glass. its nice to see you again.   It's been a long time."

He fell right into play and followed my lead. "Wow! Is this little Carole Tate?"

"Yes it is Deacon. Now that my baby is older, I can tell you a secret." Mom snickered just a bit.

"What's that?" He was struggling to keep his Christian composure.

"Well, when she was young, she had such the cutest crush on you but she didn't think I knew.   I knew alright."   She laughed. I remembered!

"Mamma! You're embarrassing me."

"Oh alright.. well I have a great idea.. Why don't you come over later for a slice of that pie of mine that you love so much?" She patted his hand in that church motherly fashion.

"I really can't. I have to take care of some things before tomorrow." He didn't look in my direction while saying these words or he would have thought twice about saying them. ***How dare he tum my mother down while I'm standing right here. I'll see about that!***

"Oh now Deacon, I'm sure you can spare a few moments of your time for my mother..." The look I gave him let him know that he better not even think about not coming.

"Well I guess I can spare some time for this beautiful woman." He loosened his tie just a bit...yeah it was definitely heating up in here. My mother blushed all over the place.

Later that afternoon, while my mother prepared a

place at the table for the Deacon, I changed into a cream sheer top and some jeans. Nothing special but the top was a little see through. I stood in the doorway behind my mother so that I was in direct view of the Deacon. I licked my lips and pinched my nipples just a little to get and keep his attention. Before I knew it, he was asking my mother if he could use the bathroom. This was perfect! *I am horny as hell and this man has held my mind for as long as I can remember. I do not give a damn how but he is giving me some of that dick before he leaves this house!*

I stood in the bathroom and waited for him.

"So what took you so long?" I said those words as I reached for him...he tried to avoid my seeking hands.

"Look I can't do this! It was an accident... it shouldn't have happened and I'm sorry."

"I'm not sorry... " was all I had to say as I pulled my shirt over my head to expose my ripe nipples, getting on my knees. He tried to pull me up but that shit was not happening. I deftly unzipped his trousers, placing his dick between my breasts and began to massage him slowly then fast. He was ready but like I said, I wasn't going nowhere until that fat dick was inches deep inside me.

I leaned over, grabbed the sink and pushed my ass back on him. He spread my pussy open so fast I could not even prepare for it. That shit was thick as hell and hard as a fucking rock! I wanted to laugh and cry at the same time!

He was talking to me the entire time, telling me how sorry he was and how we are so wrong for this but he kept on fucking me. My pussy was soaked and you could hear the splatter of my juices every time he went in and out of me. I could feel him swell up inside of me.

"Shit baby... this pussy is right. I don't want to stop. Fuck this! If you even think about giving this shit to someone else, I will fuckin kill you. You understand me? I.. will.. fuckin.. kill youuuu. Damn baby, I'm about to cuuuumm!"

He injected me with all of his liquid excitement and left nothing behind. My knees shook and we were both out of breath .

"Look you get yourself together. I have to get downstairs to your mother but this can't happen here again and don't forget what I said... you belong to me and only me.."

And with that he walked out of the bathroom. He

got very possessive very quick. The dick was great but I fuck who ever I want.

Back downstairs, the two of them were talking church and God. *Oh I was just calling God while he was ramming this pussy*.

"Baby sit down, you been running around cleaning and taking care of me. I should be taking care of you. I was telling Deacon Glass how I wanted him and the Pastor to talk to you about joining the church." She was pouring him another glass of Tea.

"Mom, I don't plan on being in town for too long so I would rather pass."

"Nonsense! The pastor will be here tonight to discuss some church business and I want you front and center." It had come out as a demand, not a request. I remained silent.

"Well Deacon.. I guess you have to get to your business. I will bake you a whole pie next time so you can take it to that pretty wife of yours."

What the hell just happened here? Did she just say wife? I didn't see a ring on his finger and he never mentioned a wife! And, as if it didn't matter that I was standing there with this confused look on my face, he turns to my mother and says..

"Maybe next time I will bring her with me.."

My mother is always trying to get me in church. I swear that's what broke her and daddy up but she acts as if it's such a big secret..shit folks get divorced every day and no one gives two fucks. The Deacon had left and left me with that same confused ass look on my face. Now the Pastor was coming.

"Baby, why don't you go upstairs and change into some more suitable clothes?"

"What's wrong with what I have on?"

"Well nothing's really wrong with it.. it's just that the deacon is a much younger, hip "today" kind of man but the Pastor is a different thing."

I understood that to mean "get upstairs and put on your little House on the Prairie dress". Well, you can't argue with mom dukes so it is what it is.

All I could hear was my mother laughing and giggling like a little school girl. When I walked to the dining room my mother asked me to bring in the coffee. I had the feeling I was being watched but I disregarded the feeling until my mother yelled for me to show the Pastor where the cabinet with the good cups were. I guess since he was tall she did not have to worry about getting a chair.

"They are right there on the left hand side."

As I reached over my head, I could feel this nigga with his dick pushed up against my ass! I should punch this nigga square in his mouth! *Hmmm..maybe this will work for me.* I saw that pretty ass car he pulled up in and I know he got a nice little account with all that money floating around. I think his wife died some time back. *Maybe I need me an old head to scratch my back when I itch. I will show that punk as deacon how to play. He wants to bring his wife over and act like my pussy ain't that shit...*

I pushed my ass out and gave a soft moan and well..I don't need to tell you what happened, but I will. His pants grew instantly and his hand started to shake. Don't ask me what that was about but I got him right where I wanted him. He was about to be a pawn in my little game. I had to make it fast before my mother came in the kitchen.

"You wanna fuck me daddy?" He swallowed air and said.."Yes"

That was all I needed to hear. *I am going to play this shit like a fuckin game of spades with me holding all trump cards and by the time I'm done, I will have both of these niggas eating out of the palm of my hands.*

"I guess you better be getting back in there before my mother comes in and sees you with your hands all in my cookie jar." This shit was gonna be easier than taking candy from a baby!

"I want you to come by the church tomorrow night. I have a meeting but I will be done by 7." He was attempting to bring his heart rate and the bulge in his pants under control.

"Daddy, how about you meet me over at that little hotel out by the airport?"

"That sounds good... I'll see you there."

For the rest of his visit, I could hear him and my mother laughing as if they were old friends until he asked about my father. This was such a hush hush topic. To this day, I still do not know why they divorced. They seemed so happy. They loved the same movies, took date night very serious and loved me. One Sunday daddy was picking us up from church, like he did each Sunday, and then one Sunday he was gone. I could tell that my mother was ready for the Pastor to leave by the way she said..

"Well Pastor, I have so much to do before getting ready for work tomorrow."

He got the message. "I understand Sister Tate. I should not have bothered. I did not mean to be a busy body.

"It's OK, you are my pastor.. if anyone can ask it's you.

I just would rather not get into the topic today." She suddenly sounded tired, old and very sad.

"Fair enough."

"Well Sister Tate, I will call you some time this week." And he was gone.

That night I couldn't sleep just thinking about Deacon Glass' fine ass but if I had to go through Pastor Holmes to get to him then....

"Baby, how was your visit with Sister Tate the other day?"

Deacon Glass was surprised that Ramona even asked about his visit. In the few years that he has visited the members of the church never once did she ever ask how someone was coming along. He felt nervous for a second but shook it off quickly and answered the question.

"Sister Tate is doing well.. she is on a high since she received that plaque at church. Yes, I would say she is doing very well."

"That's good...maybe next time I will go with you.." What was up with her!

"Sister Tate actually made that very suggestion today..." Ramona continued.

"... I have to make some runs today and I may be back a little late. I am picking up my sister, we have a dinner date. You are welcome to join us if you are freed up soon..."

"No sweetheart, you enjoy your time with your sister. Just call me in your travels and let me know how things are going and be careful. Just because you are a woman of GOD doesn't mean these folks out here are."

"I will be very careful. Love you honey." He graciously received her motherly like peek.

"Love your more Mrs. Glass.. Maybe I will take a little drive back over to sister Tate's and have some more of her wonderful pie.."

As Deacon Glass made his way up the road in the direction of the Tate home, he spotted Carole's car heading in the opposite direction. She was so busy fixing her lipstick in the mirror, she did not even notice him. He thought to himself maybe she will be back shortly but something convinced him to turn the car around and follow her. He made sure to stay at least 3 cars behind just in case she spotted him. Her car finally pulled into the parking lot of some hotel out by the airport.

"What the hell is going on here?"

He sat in his car sank down in his seat and watched to see what her next move would be. She walked into the office and came out with keys. She entered room 123 but alone. He wanted to go up and find out what was going on but waited. The next 20 minutes left him speechless and surprised. Who walks up the stairs wearing dark shades with no sun out but the PASTOR himself!

"What the fuck?!"

He felt sick to his stomach, growing angrier by the moment. How could he give a shit about whom the Pastor was nailing? He pulled out his phone and starting taking pictures of both cars and the location where they were parked.

"I just told this bitch she belonged to me. She must be taking me for a fucking joke. I got something for the both of them." Meanwhile...

"I didn't think you would show up." I sat primly with legs crossed discreetly.

"Why wouldn't I?" He asked, watching me intently.

"So what now Pastor, you gonna lay hands on me?"

"I just don't know what to say.. maybe I should just go. This is wrong on so many levels and the flesh is weak. The devil has put you in front of me as a test to my faith and I'm in need of spiritual guidance right now." The man seemed to be genuinely confused...I really didn't give a fuck.

"In the meantime daddy, let me worry about your flesh."

She slowly walked towards him with cat like moves licking her lips and thinking by *the time I finish with you I will have that Deacon so jealous he wont want anyone else but me*. Pulling her dress over her head to expose her brown body gave instant erection to the man standing before her. She walked closer and whispered in his ear.

"My pussy is so wet."

Her nipples were hard and her ass firm to the touch.   She stood in front of him and touched her toes so he could rub his growing dick against her ass. He nearly buckled once he did it.

"Let me help you out of those things daddy."

Taking off his clothes extra slow just to watch him squirm was so funny to her. When she was finished she though he wasn't as bad looking as she thought he would be and in fact his dick was bigger than she expected. That was definitely a nice surprise. Kissing the Pastor slow and laying him down on the bed gave her such a sense of power. It even seemed exciting. Climbing on top of him   and sliding down on him gave both of them a rush like never before! Her movement grew faster and she realized that she was about to cum and slowed down her rhythm.

"Oh my lord... yes baby... ride that dick just like that. Whatever you want is yours just ask for it and I will give it to you."

She heard that and started to speed up again. Maybe she was chasing the wrong man? He is in charge of everything and he ain't married. Maybe I could just fuck the Deacon one last time and then shot his shit down and make Pastor my boo.

Before she could have another thought he pulled her up with the force of two men and sat her entire ass on his face!

"Wait... no stop I have to pee. Did you hear me I have to go to the bathroom!"

She pulled away with moments to spare and ran for the bathroom with him right behind her. All of a sudden, the Pastor was in control of this situation. Turning on the shower and telling her to get in. he began to rub body wash all over her. He washed her with his bare hands and pushed her down to her knees. She took him in like a pro. Sucking him slow and then faster, allowing her tongue to dance all over him. Blowing air on it after she pulled it out drove him crazy!

"Spit on it." She looked up and gave him a smile while she spit on it repeatedly. He slapped it across her face and played keep away with her tongue until she begged for it...

*I can't believe this shit! I have to get out of here until I can figure out what I'm going to do about this. This fuckin whore! Bad enough she got me all caught up and now my Pastor. Naw shit ain't going down like that. Who the fuck do she think she is? That's just why I don't trust bitches.*

Pulling off, he made up in his mind he would wait nearby her home to question her about what she was up to and why.

When she finally pulled up in the driveway, he wanted to grab her by her throat and choke her until she begged for mercy.

"So where were you?" She nearly jumped out her skin which gave the Deacon some small satisfaction.

"Oh my God... you scared me! What are you

doing out here?"

"I was waiting for you. I didn't want to knock on the door...I wanted us to take a ride." "Well how about if we go tomorrow?" She was actually a little tired.

"Come on baby don't be like that...Come on."

After thinking about it for a second she thought why not.

"I really need to be getting back soon though, I can't pull an all-nighter because I won't be staying that long. I have to get back to New York and work."

After about 10 minutes, he pulled over to the side of the road.

"Open your legs." He demanded!

"What?"

"Did I stutter? Open your legs bitch!" She just didn't know how close she was to getting that ass beat!

"Who the fuck you calling a bitch nigga?" He grabbed her by the throat and stuck his free hand up her skirt in order to feel her pussy. It was soaked as if she never bothered to wash after the good ole pastor came all up in her.

"Get off me!" She screamed and pushed but it was useless.

"Bitch shut the fuck up! Pastor Holmes can get it

all day but I told you that you belong to me now and that's how you do me?"

The look on her face said it all.

"I got pictures. I followed your ass today. What would your mother think about all of this? How would she ever be able to hold her head up in church again? She would be heart broken. I don't want you to see him again. That's it...You did what you did but I will be watching you and if you slip again, your mother will have to move away."

After he made his point, he lowered her head down on his dick until she began to gag. He made sure to keep her head in place until she swallowed ever bit of it. When the episode was over and they were headed back to her mother's, she finally spoke.

"So what does this mean for us now? Ok, you know I'm sleeping with him what about it? Your married.. what do you care who I open my legs to?!"

"I just can't have you fuckin him. You belong to me and that's that. As long as you remember that, everything will be fine but the minute you act like you forgot well, that's another story. Do we understand one another? I want that sweet ass whenever I feel like it and if I think that someone else is up in it..it's a problem."

She was now exhausted and totally disgusted. Had she bitten off more than she could chew.

"Look I need to go in. We can talk about this another time.."

"Just don't forget what I said, now give me a kiss." And with that, he was gone.

Her mother was waiting. "Hey sweetie, how was your day?

"It was good mom. I really miss being in Philly, but work calls so you know I have to be going in a few days. I was thinking I could take you out tomorrow. What do you think? You up for it? We could go to the zoo like when I was a little girl only this time you don't need to hold my hand or pick me up to see the animals then we could go somewhere and eat."

"I would love that." Her mother's smile was infectious.

"Cool! Well tonight we will just chill, watch Scandal and order pizza."

"Oh baby, I miss you in this house."

"Mommy don't start getting corny on me... besides you can come to New York with me for a while and keep me company. You know I'm looking for a house now. It's time for me to move out of Aunt Dorothy's house. I never understood why you sent me there in the first place but I guess you had your reasons. Don't get me wrong, she is great! It's more like we're friends. The point is, I'm a grown woman now and I have a good job and a career, so its time for me to leave another nest. I have plenty of space for you mom." She meant every word; she would love to have her mother in New York with her.

"No, I will stay right here in the city of Brotherly Love and Sisterly Affection. Besides, I have my own friends and my schedule. I stay busy. Besides, what if I had a boyfriend?"

"Mom that topic is not up for discussion." They both broke into hilarious laughter.

It felt good to sit and watch TV.all night with my mom, talking like teenagers. I finally took a deep breath and attempted to clear my head of today's events. *I have to figure out a way to keep the Pastor on a short leash but keep the Deacon off my ass. I guess I had better think about that later for now.. Get Em Kerri Washington!*

The next day couldn't have been more perfect. The sun was shining with the air clear for some reason. I loved this little block I grew up on. It actually was completely filled with white people years ago until they got tired of all the black folks moving in but everyone was older and had jobs and now their children were grown. You still had your drama but it was low-level drama. The previous year, I'd had security doors and windows put on along with an alarm system to which I also had the password. Mom still drove and had her circle of friends, so she was a very busy woman. Going to the zoo made me think of my dad, though I never said a word. We just walked, talking and acting as if he'd never existed. Our day was    filled with funny stories, laughter and watching people act crazy. There was a moment when she asked if there was a special man in my life. I told her no and that was that.

By the end of the day, we were both tired and beat. I couldn't wait to get my clothes off; l needed a hot bath and a glass of wine.

"Mom, I was thinking about getting in the tub. Do you need to use if first?"

"No baby, I'm good.. go right ahead."

*This has been a crazy week. I came here wanting one man and getting another who has been a total surprise all the way around.* I could control all of this if I planned right. *Who the hell does that fool think he is being married and having me whenever he wants and then getting pissed and acting crazy because I'm fuckin someone else. I need to figure this one out and fast...*

All night she tossed and turned thinking about both men and the possibilities. If only for one moment, she could have both at the same time. It was as if the thought gave her power and pleasure all at once. She could feel the moisture seeping through her panties. Her satin sheets made for the perfect effect to her fantasy. The soft material slid across her nipples and gently between her legs. The dream became so real that she woke herself up by way of accidental moans. She could not return to sleep afterwards. She was obsessed and before she left Philly, she would have them both.

_____

# Secret Meetings

"You wanted to see me Pastor?" He wondered if the Pastor really knew.

"Deacon Glass, I watched you grow in this church from a boy to a man. Your father started this church and his dream was that one day you would take over and run things and lead the flock. I'm thinking of retiring early, doing some traveling and I wanted to talk to you before going to the board with this. I think its time for you to take your place at the front of the Alter. What do you think?" Glass hadn't expected this.

"Wow! I don't really know what to say, do I have some time to think about it?"

"Sure you do. I just figured you are young, you and your wife have good jobs, you are well respected in the community and it's your birthright. It's time to get some new blood in here. By the way, I have an offer to make and I want you to consider this as well." Here comes the bullshit...

"What's that?" Glass asked cautiously.

"I want you to stop following me and taking pictures."

The look on Deacons Glass' face was of sheer surprise but it quickly turned to curiosity. If he knew that then what else did he know?

"Listen, I have nothing to lose but a little dignity. However, you on the other hand, your wife, your father's church, everything. I'm sure we can come to some type of understanding or compromise to make us both feel better."

He definitely had my attention.

"I'm listening." The good Pastor had nothing in mind but a good old fashion threesome. He felt as if they both were entitled to it. A Right of Passage or an initiation, if you will, and she would be the sexual sacrifice.   By the end of the meeting, both men agreed.

---

# The Call

"Why are you calling me this early? You must miss this ass already?" Carole yawned into the phone.

"Can you meet me at the same place as before room 234 this time? I will be there in an hour and wear something sexy."

"How about nothing at all?"

"You sure know how to make an old man feel good."

"You are not old first off and second you got these young niggas beat by a long shot. I will see you soon."

As the Pastor hung up the phone, he could see Deacon Glass sitting in awe.

"I still can't believe that we are about to do this."

"Honestly this is something we all go through when we take this step.. it's like a bonding brotherhood.

Your father and I had this same ritual with a woman of the church. I know your mother was a great woman but who are we to be changing something that has become a part of us since before we could even understand it."

---

# The Knock

As she waited for Pastor Holmes to answer the door, she thought she spotted the Deacon's car. She thought to herself what the hell is he doing here? There was really no need to think any further, she already knew what was about to happen and she didn't even have to plan it. She took a deep breath and fixed her hair. One last thing to do was to push the record button on her device so that the Deacon's wife could hear every little whisper. Carole had decided to pay her a visit the night before and inform her of what was going on since she now her eyes were set on Pastor Holmes. She paid Carole to get everything on tape so she could divorce him and take everything he had; even his fathers' church. She had agreed and now it was time to get the job done plus have some fun.

"Hey daddy, I missed you" she said as she put her bag in the chair.

"Hello Carole."

She never even turned to acknowledge the deacon, just walked to the middle of the room, dropping her coat to the floor to reveal she wore nothing underneath. Both men were going over every bit of her body with their eyes as if they had seen heaven. Walking towards the bed, she took both hands and spread open her ass cheeks to let both of them know she was serious. She made sure to call each one by first name. Lyle was Pastor Holmes and Mark was the deacon.

"Mark, eat that pussy baby. Make me moan. Lyle, fuck me harder daddy!"

For the next 2 hours, the two men took turns sucking, slapping, fucking, and teasing every single inch of her. She was exhausted and had to be carried to the shower where they continued until there was a knock at the door...

They could hear the key being placed in the lock. It could only be the housekeeper.

"We don't need anything... we are fine."

As the keys stop jiggling and door opening made that pop sound, both men became frantic!

"Hello Lyle, hello Mark.." She was so calm and cool.

Both men were standing frozen in the middle of the floor with hard dicks and racing hearts. Sister Sue Glass, the Deacon's wife, stood in the door with a camera in one hand and tape recorder in the other. She waited a beat of a minute before she played back the last few seconds of their threesome.

"Before I tell you what I want from both of you, we have some unfinished business.."

She walked to the bed, dropped her coat and spread her legs...

# Ride and Die

She taps her soft pack of Newport then pulls one out. Every week she tells her self that this will be her last cigarette. She lights it up and takes a drag.    She allows the smoke to fill her lungs.    It relaxes her before a hopefully long night of work. She blows smoke rings as she watches the movement of the new booty on the stroll tonight. She loves to see when fresh fish hits the comer. She never feels threatened by new competition because she is seasoned in the game and has a nice list of regulars that include police officers, lawyers and even a local politician.

In her years, she has managed to stay away from drugs, pimps, and visits to the clinic for penicillin. Even her apartment was very nice and well kept. Every month she would send her mother some money to help financially cover any and all expenses to help raise her daughter.

Trishella, who called herself Irish was always smart but for some reason got caught up in this life and has never looked back. She had practiced her walk, her talk, and her seductive voice. She spots a new car on the block, pushes her breast up, pulls her skirt up, and approaches   her mark.

"Hey baby you looking for a good time."

He hides his razor between his legs and with a sinister voice...

"Your place or mine?" Both individuals with a plan for the night but two very different directions. She felt uneasy about this trick but money had to be made and she was short the rent this month.

As he opens the door for her, she pulls her skirt up just enough for him to see that she's not wearing any panties. For a split second, he was so transfixed by what was not under her skirt, he found himself growing with pleasure. His thought went instantly from driving down the next dark alley and slashing her throat to pushing her head so far down on his dick that she would choke on contact and as soon as she began to choke, he would kill her and dump her lifeless body in the trash.

"So where you from honey?"

She liked to ask a few questions right out the gate just in case she had to remember something or give the cops any information.

"Virginia." He wasn't necessarily interested in idle chit chat.

"What are you doing in Philly?"

"Just passing through, what's it to you?"
Talk about attitude.

"Nothing... just making conversation."

"So what's your name?" Finally

"You can call me Irish."

"Well Irish, is there a fee for this ride or is it free?" She almost laughed in his face but something in his demeanor made her think twice.

"Honey, ain't shit free but pain and suffering and it's plenty of that to go around. As for this pussy right here.. It's 20 for a blow job, 100 for pussy and I don't do anal but if it's what you want then it's an extra 20."

" So how much for the whole night?"

"Well now baby, you just want to spend all that bill money on me huh?"

"I want a good time and I want it done right, that's all. I asked around I was told that you are the best and that's what I am paying for. .. The Best."

He pulled out a stack of hundred dollar bills.

"Baby, I am going to fuck you crazy. When I am finished with you, no one else will be able to touch you because you will belong to Irish..."

He didn't seem impressed or convinces.

"We will see about that but you didn't

answer the question. How much for the whole night?" He didn't seem to have much of a sense of humor either.

"I see you're a business man.. hmm.. I like that. It's 500.00 sweetheart. Can you handle that?"

The trick leafed through his stash and Trish lit up like a Christmas tree in the window of Macy's waiting for Santa to come down the street giving gifts to all the little good boys and girls. She thought about waiting until he went to sleep and taking him for every penny of it but she reminded herself it would put her in the same category with all these others hoes that made it bad for hard working girls such as herself. If she handled this the way she should, he would definitely be back for more and most likely tell his friends about her.

"So where are we going or is that a secret?"

"I'll tell you what... how about we go grab something to eat and then pick a place?" He was already becoming irritated with her but nothing was going to keep him from getting her alone.

"It's your money daddy but remember this shit ain't coming off your tab. You wanted to stuff your face. I am just along for the ride. I'm one of those ride or die chicks that they talk about on the rap videos."

How funny he thought this was but later for that. He pulled out his roll of money and peeled off $400.00 dollars and passed them over with a smile.

"We cool now?" It was immediately stuff in her secret bra compartment.

"Oh, we real cool now daddy. I like the way you do business. Let me take you to a little spot on Broad and Fairmount where we take all of our visitors. The food is cheap but good and you can watch them cooking your meal. You never know if some dirty white boy decided not to wash his hands and I don't play that shit."

"So you care if he washes his hand but you can suck his dick?" This was mind-boggling to him.

As they approached the dimly lit restaurant, Trish could see one of her old tricks sitting in the booth with some fresh fish. This chick looked older than her mother so she smiled in his direction just to make him mad. She even put on a super sexy walk as they went by. She could feel him watching her ass and she loved every minute of it. He'd tried to short her some money for services rendered and she'd kicked him so hard in his nuts that he thought she left the print of her shoe tip on his balls. He could not pee straight for two days.

Trish was well versed in the streets and had been on her own since she was 14. Now 26, she could easily be considered an old head to the new girls coming out. She could also fight, something she unfortunately learned quick walking the streets.

As they sat down, Trish leaned in and whispered..

"I could fuck you right here on this table in front of all these nice people if you like?"

Though that sounded great to him, he told her they would take care of all of that and then some once they got back to the spot but for now he was hungry.

"So what would you like?"

"Why don't you order for me daddy and I will go to the little girls room."

"Don't take too long."

Trish walked down the path to the restroom; as she entered, she was grabbed from behind! He had one hand over her moth so she couldn't scream and the other over her breast.

"Bitch I knew I would run into your sooner or later.." he said with a low growl. "Come here!"

As he began to pull up her skirt and expose

her already glistening treasure, he could feel her laughing at him. He removed his hand from over her mouth in order to hear what she had to say.

"Come on nigga... do what you gotta do. I see that old ass bitch out there ain't gonna satisfy you like I did."

At that second, he sat Trish up on the bathroom sink, starting to eat as if she were his last meal on earth. He sucked her with aggression! Every slurp and smack of his lips was followed by gentle fight him all the long pushing her ass closer to his open mouth.

"Tell me you want me to suck it harder and I will suck this shit off and you won't have anything left for your little friend out there."

The more she tried to talk the further he stuck his tongue inside. Her head rolled back and leaned up against the mirror. Her legs open while her love squirted over his tongue and moans grew with intensity. Trish was pushing herself as far into his mouth as possible. Her ass moving with such force she accidentally turned on the motion sink.

As water begins to run, she can see in the mirror her trick standing in the doorway watching it all. At first she felt nervous and thought she had just fucked up a lot of money with this one act of vengeance..To her pleasant surprise, she looked down and saw his dick was in his hands and a big fuckin dick it was. She smiled when she saw it. And that made her work extra hard to cum. The two of them locked eyes and never looked away as she talked to him through her moans. So far her current conquest was so caught up that he never saw anyone else in the room with them. She even pretended that she and her new suitor were alone.

The more she moaned, the more he jerked and stroked his dick until it excited her so much she came as she watched him spill his pleasure all in the palm of his hand. Her body began to relax as he slid out of the door.

"Let's say I ditch that bitch at the table and you get rid of the sucka you wit and we make this a night?" Her juices shined brightly on this dude's swollen lips.

"I can't baby because that cat is paid up until tomorrow and I ain't about to blow it."

She pulled down her skirt and left him in the bathroom, returning to her seat as if nothing had happened. She looked down at her plate to see a juicy steak, baked potato and cabbage. She couldn't wait to put her fork in all of it.

"So are you going to tell me your name or shall I give you a nick name?" She was trying not to talk with her mouth full of steak; it wasn't working too well.

"My name is Randolph." She stopped chewing for just a minute.

"Randolph, are you shittin me?! That's some serious white boy shit... Can I call you Randy or Royce?" No way was a man with all that dick supposed to be called Randolph.

"Royce sounds good but how did you come up with that?" He could care less what she called him as long as she satisfied his appetite.

"I don't know... it just sounds much better than Randolph or Randy."

"I guess Royce it is then."

"I appreciate dinner. So you like to watch?"

"I actually came in to see what was taking you so long but then I noticed the woman sitting by herself and well, I put two and two together."

"So what did you think?" For the life of her, Irish couldn't understand why she asked that question.

"I think I want to hurry up out of here! Waitress can we get this to go?" This one really talked too much!

Once they found a motel, they couldn't get each other's clothes off fast enough. Royce stood back and watched her body in the moonlight. He thought how gorgeous she was and so unlike any of the other women that worked the streets. She had a softness to her that was uncommon in her line of work. She spoke so softly; she actually made him feel like he mattered.

"Whats the matter Royce?" He was watching her strangely. He was definitely NOT her normal trick.

"Nothing... I just think you should be married to someone making them happy, not walking the streets."

"Well I guess I should say thank you."

She walked towards him slowly, like some mythological creature. With elegance and grace. Like a queen that was being presented to her royal subjects. She sat in the middle of the bed and opened her legs to welcome him in. He reached in his pocket and pulled out a glow in the dark pink condom. It barely fit over his massive rod. When he reached the bed he flipped her over and entered her doggy style. She felt nothing but pain at first and then it started to feel really good. Her pussy grabbed him back each time he pulled out a little.

There was a nonstop energy that this man possessed. She had never had a trick kiss her so deeply and continuously repeat 'I love you' in her ear. She almost forgot this was a job. She let him take over her body which is something she had never done or considered until now. He was strong and smelled good. This was such a turn on. It was the best night she'd in a long time.

They moved to the floor and then to the shower were she tried to get all of him in her mouth but he was really hung and each time she gagged, he held her there as if he wanted her to choke on his size. From the shower to the table he continued to feast on her. He had the energy of some unseen force but she refused to give in. Her body opened wide for him and whatever he wanted to do with her. She felt the urge to cum and was at the height of climax. his lips softly kissing her nipples as they grew hard... her legs trembling.

She suddenly felt a sharp, cold, rush to her mid section. Lifting her head was all she could do to see the large blade enter her again and again before her eyes closed for the final time with this final thought, *I knew there was something wrong with this trick the moment I saw him. ..*

As Royce wiped the blood from the knife and began to clean the room, he felt rejuvenated and powerful. It would only be a matter of time before he finally came across the woman that    turned trick after trick in front of him. That sold him to a pimp..That left him in an abandoned house to take care of himself. Each one of these whores represented her. Each one represented his....**MOTHER**.

# Vampire Freak

As I stand here and think of each one of them, a sense of pleasure and purpose covers me. It is nearly dawn and I must return soon to my place of dwelling. I guess you could call me a throwback to the days of old. I must admit that I am staying out longer as the years fly by. The night has a way of clearing your mind and allowing you to see things for what they really are. I love the crisp taste of night. The creatures that come out. The moon and the stars talk to one another. They talk about life on planet earth. Earth, this wonderful spectacle of a planet. So much misery and pain yet so much promise. I love the night. But as I said light is beginning to come out of its deep slumber and I must go. I long for the day when I can watch the sun come up and open its arms to new beginnings.. I wanted to feel the sun on my skin and smell them, all of them. They say that their smell is intoxicating and alluring beyond understanding. I have also been warned that they are very deceiving and if you should find yourself having urges and feelings that are not comprehensible well that means you are falling in love and that is devastation and destruction lurking in the shadows for you. My father and his father before him fell victim to this and I will make sure that it doesn't happen to me.. I will be smarter than them. I know what to look for and I know what my mission is. They are the weak and we are the strong!I have no friends but lots of acquaintances. I like to be social for two reasons: (1) It makes people want to be around me more and (2) It makes people want to be around me more...So, in reality there is only one reason.

Men love to be around me because I have a beautiful smile and a wonderful personality ... Ha! It's because I am a beautiful chocolate coated sistah built like a muthafuckin brick house. My ass, hips, breasts, and lips are what they are after. The women, they hang around because I live like a rock star and I know where the guys are. I couldn't care less about the reasons but what I do care about is how people disappeared without a trace and if I am not careful I could slip up. There have been many in my family who have slipped up and ended up dead because they fell in love and lost control. I know the pit falls and I am much smarter than any one from my family tree. Well you and I will talk later, for now I must hurry the sun is harking.. And contrary to what some may believe, this beautiful black skin can't handle the sun. Who am I? My name is Helena and I am the daughter of **VAMPIRES**...

---

# Anthony

From my rear view mirror on a Friday night fixing my lipstick, we make eye contact. Just a typical weekend getting ready to hang out with some of my friends, excuse me, associates. We were a group of four and we were ready to party. I had just purchased myself a 2014 all black something off of the show room floor. I was always bad with the names of cars and it didn't matter much what the name was because it was a big pretty bitch! The salesman promised me that when I stepped out of this people would want to be me..Ha ha ha I liked that. He made me laugh but he made me a believer and if I didn't believe then, I would believe later. As soon as I pulled up to my Ritten House Square apartment, all eyes were on me. First and foremost my neighbors were still trying to figure out if I was some type of celebrity since I was the only black person living in the building. Don't get me wrong, they were not branding sheets and burning crosses but the way they said hello with questioning eyes, if they said hello at all, spoke volumes. One older woman had the nerve to ask me if I was the care taker for some rich white man in the building! I started to take her into a dark comer and drain every ounce of blood from her old ass but I never eat where I sleep.

Anyway, I went to my closet and took out this little black tight fitting dress with the back out and little to the imagination. I didn't give a fuck because it was a bait and hook type of night and I had not fed in two weeks. I refused to be like others and kill innocent animals to spare the life of some cruel monster of a human. I got in my car and one by one picked up my female associates. I had to say that they all looked gorgeous but they still had nothing on me. I must admit, I considered turning all of them because I could see us going through cities devouring everything in sight. Sitting at the stop light waiting for the green was when I noticed him watching me. And to be sure I waved to the mirror and he responded by flashing his lights. Got One! I immediately pulled over and got out of my car so he could watch me walk over to him. I read his eyes but his mouth said...

"Damn baby, can I help you carry that ass?"

"Anytime you want." He looked at me with a curious concern.

I leaned into his car window and said we are about to hit this club on Spring Garden Street, if you want to go with us I will pay your way in and drinks are on me. He had a smile on his face.

"By the ,my name is Anthony and what's yours?"

"My name is Helena so what will it be?"

I slowly walked back to my car and gave my girls a wink as we began to pull off. When I looked back he was following our every move. By the time we got into the club it was packed! Standing room only but I have a way with words so I got us a VIP section and ordered a few bottles of Cristol. I have no idea why these humans love this so much. There is nothing more delicious than a scared man.

While my girl were on the floor bumping and grinding as hard as they could, I turned to Anthony, opening my legs so he knew I wanted some. He licked his lips and came close. I slowly unzipped his pants, lowering my head in his lap. Mmm... he was so hard and his dick was silky. I started to go faster and faster until he tried to pull my head up from excitement but it was too late. I had already put him in a trans state so I dug my fangs into his dick. By morning he would be a loyal subject. By day, he would carry on as usual; by night, he would be the first of my followers begging me to use him.

---

# Sam

Poor Sam.. he was so nervous the day we met. I almost didn't want to turn him but who am I to go against the natural order of things?

I was walking through Fairmount Park late one night. I could not resist. The moon was so close to the earth that I could feel my panties getting moist. Though I am a vampire, I am still a woman and that full moon made me hunger even more. It was as if the dark sky was my lover and the moon its pleasure toy for me. I was now in the Strawberry Mansion area of Philly. A car slowed, the driver yelling out to me.

"How much?" I knew exactly what he meant and I planned to have some fun with him.

"Well daddy it depends on what you want."

Sam looked me up and down, starting to drool.

"I have 50.00 dollars in my pocket." I smiled

"That won't get you a lot but it will get you enough to make you happy."

He pulled over to the side of the road just under some trees so it would be hard for the cops to spot us. I attempted to unzip his pants but he reclined the seat and put his face on my thigh to let me know what was to happen first. I was pleasantly surprised at how unselfish he was. I liked that.

He kissed his way up my cave and placed his face so far in my pussy that I thought he was trying to climb inside of me and come out my mouth. It felt so damn good, all I could do was hold his head in place and moan for dear life. In all my centuries, I have never come across a human with such skill. He licked every bit of cum and sucked until more ran down his lips. I knew this was his fetish. He sounded like a dog lapping up water from a bowl.

With each lick, my body shook and that is when it happened, as my mouth was open and I began moaning louder, my fangs began to glisten and grow! I don't know why Sam chose that moment to look up but when he did, he jumped back so fast and hard, I thought he would go through the door. His eyes were wide as fear fell over his face. I made it a point to control him at that moment in order to let him know he was in no danger; that he and I would be together. I was too wet and still craving his oral ministrations and so I told him to finish, he obeyed. His mouth was fantastic! I pushed every bit of juice out of my body for him. I climbed on top of him, finding my stride.

As I rode, faster and harder, my fangs came out again and this time, I bit into him. The feeling of blood running down my lips and past my tongue made my hunger for my prey intensify. He had no idea, at that very moment, he was actually the one in control. I needed him to understand my world was so much better than his. He was now drained of blood and cum. He belonged to me...

\*\*\*\*\*\*\*\*\*\*\*\*

I have not always been this way. I had a wonderful life at one point in my past though that has been many, many years ago.. I have always been a vampire but I walked through this life as any other normal teenager at that time.

During those times, women were more like cattle and men were like gods. They made and broke the rules when they saw fit and there were no laws to keep them in order. It was a time when white men owned black slaves and you were either a Yankee or Southerner.

It was a warm summer day and I was just turning 17. My parents had just worked Master Bradley's plantation and were overseeing the slaves that worked in the field. They called my parents

House Niggas..They were both very fair skinned with sandy brown hair. I never understood that especially since I was the color of deep chocolate? I remember asking my parents why we didn't just use our special powers to go from plantation to plantation, killing the slave owners and freeing the black people?

"Baby, one day you will understand why it is important to our way of life to allow these people to take care of themselves. They have special ways of killing vampires and we need to fit right in. Not only that, if these people of ours found out what we were... they would betray us the first chance they get." My father was adamant about this.

My mother supported my father.

"Your father is right so say nothing and do nothing. Our time is coming and you will know then what role you play in all of this."

In the meantime, I enjoyed sleeping in the big house and getting all of that extra food always left over. My parents would remind me every night that I had to grow strong so when the time came I could do what I needed to. The big house always smelled of peach cobbler and spice because my mother was

were spread open and I knew I was in big trouble. I could most likely beat him and both of his cousins but that would mean that I would have to kill all three boys and mamma and daddy had warned me of the special ways they kill vampires. I thought what good is having these special abilities if I can't protect myself when I need to? My parents would be sold and/or killed and I would meet the same fate.

Thomas had this look in his eyes I'd never seen and before I could blink, he had his trousers down. He pounced, immediately pushing up inside of me! It hurt so badly I tried to scream but his cousin Roy covered my mouth. He laughed and I could see the saliva dripping from his lips. His teeth were smaller than those of a growing boy; they looked like little knives. I could hear him say..

"Dang cousin, save some for me! Hot damn you told me this nigger was pretty and you sure told the truth. They don't look like this at home. It was worth the trip. This is going to be one hell of a summer. Darkie you may as well get use to this."

Finally, when Roy couldn't take any more waiting, he pushed Thomas off of me and barely got his pants down before he started rubbing his pecker all over my breast and telling me that I would barely be able to walk when they were done. I cried, kicked, and bit them but nothing seemed to work and no one came to help me. I think I passed out for a minute but when I opened my eyes Thomas and Roy were laughing and out of breath. Each one took me and pulled my legs so far apart, I thought they would rip them from my body. The last one to get on top of me was Jack. He was dirty looking and smelled bad. He smelled as if he had been sleeping with pigs. He pulled down his pants and I swear it looked like two peckers in one. It was so big and fat that I screamed so loud that I felt the earth shake! It must have scared all three of them because the look on their faces was as if they'd seen a ghost.

All of a sudden, I felt energy come over me like I had never felt before! I felt strong and powerful! I felt extremely hot and excited about something. Between my legs was on fire and I felt as if I wanted them all at one time! The scratches and bruises covering my body were disappearing inssimultaneously. Every sound in the woods became louder. Each blade of grass became a brighter green and the smells, however sweet, began to overwhelm me. As I took in and became a part of nature, my rapists stood in astonishment at what they were witnessing. I took a deep breath and opened my eyes as it seemed, for the first time ever...

I locked eyes with Roy. Though he attempted to back up, it was not fast enough. I leaped on him as if I were a cougar catching its prey! I could smell the fear in him and it aroused me in such a way, unlike any other feeling I'd ever known. I licked him from his ear to his Adams apple where I dug my fangs into him and ripped out his voice box! It tasted so good, I immediately grabbed the other side of his neck and opened it up, exposing the beautiful color and flesh. It felt so sexual to me and I wanted more. Maybe this was the feeling they all got when taking me? If so, then as animals, we share in the delight of someone else's pain. His body had died some time ago but it shook with such magnificent movement.

Jack closed his eyes because he knew there was no escaping..I stuck my tongue through the center of his chest and drained every bit of blood from his body until he was a gray as clay. Finally it was Thomas's turn..He cried and begged but I had the taste of blood on my lips and there was no turning back.

"Ssh, don't cry... It's only going to hurt for a little while. You didn't think twice about hurting me! In fact, you enjoyed it and invited friends! How dare you!"

I looked him in the eyes and without speaking he was my slave. He did as I said without me actually saying a word...

As he lay on the ground helpless, I slowly walked towards him. I am sure the sinister look in my eyes told him he would not live to see another day. But what I had for him was a fate worse than death. I wanted him to live long enough to see everyone and everything that he loved die. I wanted him to know that he would live because I allowed it and what I commanded of him is what would be done.

My brown body glistened and the sweet aroma of blood was splattered all over me. I climbed on top of him and opened up my walls and smothered him with all of my womb. I bounced up and down on him so hard that I became the rapist and not the raped. I went faster and faster! I kissed him and bit his lip until it bled and when he couldn't take any more I put my hot mouth over his swollen cock and bit into it until he was completely drained ..I began to shake and get excited all over again. This time I realized that I was having an orgasm. I pulled the bodies into the water and cleaned myself up and went on with my day as if nothing had happened.

Back on the plantation, Master Bradley was looking everywhere for his son and nephews. He had all the slaves lined up screaming and yelling at them to find his family before dark. Hours passed and soon the hounds were called out; the hunt was on. Finally the men came back with the grim discovery of the bodies. The talk was that no human being could have done this. It **had** to be the work of wild animals. That night, for the first time, I saw Master Bradley cry. He yelled at the moon and cursed God. He went from cabin to cabin beating men, women and children until he was too tired to do anything. My parents came to me and asked me if I knew anything about what happened to the three young men.

As we talked, I saw fear sweep across my mother's face as she said to my father...

"She's telling us a lie; I see it in her eyes.. She killed those boys..."

She began to weep and that's when my father began packing our things.

"Tonight we leave."

We could hear the screaming from cabins down the line. The next cabin to have its door kicked in was ours...My mother leaped to her feet and grabbed Master Bradley, ripping his head from his body and contrary to what the history books say, this was the uprising, the killing of slave owners on different plantations. It was **vampires**.... not Nat Turner.

We traveled up north; it was a whole new world but by that time, I had an appetite for blood. The blood of men in particular. My hatred for men had grown and I would make them pay. They...meaning any man daring to cross my path. I have watched the world change over the years and it has become much easier now to quench my thirst. My parents were both killed by a priest some years ago and I fled. One day I will go back and find that priest but for now, I am a creature of the night in search of a frightening fuck.

---

# Slick

For now I had plans and they included my two latest victims or as I call them rookies. My favorite season was fast approaching. Fall..

I love the city of Philadelphia in the fall. The colors are so beautiful. The leaves turn orange and brown. The air seems to be cleaner and people are in a rush to get indoors. It's usually around this time that women get pregnant. I have often wondered what it would feel like to be with child; however, because I was raped some hundreds of years ago something happened to my body that has kept me from doing so. When I was younger, I didn't think vampires could have babies but then, how does that explain my existence? I have long since worried about that but tonight I have been invited to a costume party and I am going as a...Vampire.

I decided to take Sam with me. I like Sam or maybe I like Sam's tongue. I'm not sure which but tonight there will be some new rookies on my team and when I'm done, I will have this city right where I want her.

Sam was such a puppy but he allowed me to play and recruit as I needed. I could tell by the look in his eyes he wanted to take me in the middle of the dance floor when he spotted me dancing with the guy I'd just met. He called himself Slick. Yeah corny right? Didn't matter one bit because he was arrogant and cocky and for that reason alone, he would join my team.

I paid for his drink and told him I had just broken up with my boyfriend of three years, catching him in bed with another woman. For some reason men think this story is the opening of legs.

"Damn girl a Nigga got to be out his fucking mind to cheat on you."

I smiled a fake smile and let him whisper in my ear. Next he put his hand on my thigh and when he saw that I didn't stop him, he slid it up my skirt. I never moved so now my eyes began to roll to the back of my head a little as he fucked me with his three fingers. Suddenly he pulled them out licking them slowly.

"Why don't we take this behind that curtain over there... my man is the owner and well.." He really did think he was SLICK! Ha!

"If your man is the owner then he should have an office."

His eyes lit up as he nodded towards the barmaid and whispered in her ear. In the next moment, we were walking towards the back to a dark room with soft plush carpet and the thump of music shaking the walls. I didn't even get in the door before Slick tore my skirt and had me bending over the desk eating my ass out. He slurped and sucked while I pushed my ass back. His fingers slid in and out of my pussy and he plucked my clit until it became swollen. As he turned me over to put his dick in my mouth, the door flung open and there stood Sam watching.

"Yo, get the fuck outta here muthafucka!"

Sam did not move. I looked up at Slick, telling him that he was with me and that it was OK. He looked confused but when he saw Sam walk over to the table and hold my mouth open for him to get all of his dick inside, he got excited all the more. They took turns pushing, pulling and sucking my nipples. They talked to one another while they came all over my stomach and face. Slick went to shake the last bit of cum out and that's when I dug my teeth into him. I put them through his skin and he froze like a statue. Sam jerked himself off while I moaned and now there were three.

As I mentioned earlier, I still couldn't watch the sun come up but I was getting closer every day. I needed my rest after a night like this so I headed for the door. I couldn't help but notice the two sets of eyes that watched me as I walked from the back of the club to the front door. I felt very vulnerable for a second and cold as if someone had just opened up my coat and let winter inside me. I brushed it off, chalking it up to my little tryst I'd just had in the back. Sam was so loyal. He drove me home and waited for me to lock my door. It was as if we were human beings for a moment in time. I can't understand why that made me feel good. (You humans are so lucky).

## Trish and Tracey

The night I met my two so-called home girls, they'd been hatin on me from the bar while I was up in VIP with this dude from up Erie Ave. He was getting paid and he had money to spend. I wasn't at all interested in his paper because I could make him hand his entire Empire over to me with just one look. What I did enjoy was the attention these bitches were given me.

While we were sitting there about to order another bottle of Cristol, Trish walks over, introducing herself to dude. I'm sitting there like *did this bitch just disrespect m*e? Dude turns and looks at me as if to say *is she serious*? After I shrugged my shoulders, I guess he figured it was OK.

"Whassup ma, my name is Trizz, what can I do for you? He asked with a raised brow.

"Well, my girl and I wanted to know if you were that dude from the video they aired tonight?" She tried to put her chest in his chest as she leaned in.

I sat thinking to myself *that's where I know this nigga from... I saw him last night on the rap station. Ok, now I get it.* Since she wanted to show her ass and act as if I wasn't there, I was gonna really make her show it publicly.

As soon as I made eye contact with Tracey, I put her right under. She was so easy to put in a trance. As she walked up, she introduced herself to Trizz and sat down. As soon as I had them both spellbound, I turned to Trizz to let him know just who the fuck was truly in charge, whispering "this is for you daddy..."

His face registered utter confusion as I sat back, opened my legs and on cue Trish came face first into me. Her lips thick and warm. She was so gentle. She made little slurping sounds while I rubbed my fingers through her hair. Trizz sat watching rubbing his dick until he had to get in on the action. Trish...Tracey...Trizz...The three T's.

Tracey slid her pussy down on him slow and hard. She bounced slowly while she reached over and pushed Trish's head further into me. I looked over and could see Trizz watching me shove my wetness into her face as if I had a dick.

"Damn baby I love you."

I leaned over and kissed him deep and hard but I didn't give two shits about what he was saying. He played me and that is unforgivable. I said to Tracy in a low soft tone..

"Get up bitch."

He gave me a look of excitement and curiosity. His dick was wet, hard, and waiting.

"What are you doing baby?"

"First off , I ain't your baby... now sit back and enjoy the show."

Now Tracy stood up on the red sofa in VIP with her skirt up and her panty-less cunt in my mouth. I could taste every bit of his dick. She glided that clean shaven skin up and down my face while bouncing on my tongue.

As Trish begged for me to cum in her mouth, I forced Trizz to watch unable to move. His dick spoke for him as it began to ooze, running down the sides of his shaft like a slowly erupting volcano. I saw that and immediately made my way over to him, bit into it while he came.   Blood and cum filled my mouth. He now belonged to me. When I was done, Trish and

Tracy were on their backs wondering what just happened. They had no idea but they now yearned for me and I loved every bit of it.

Trish and Tracey are not the only girls on my team.I have a few more that we roll with but these are the only two that I take out and play with when I get bored.   They are so weak minded. The others well.. they are just for show. As I said in the beginning, they pulled mad niggas.

My night was starting out fine or so I thought.  Once again  I  felt  that  strange uncomfortable feeling and this time it had me a little more paranoid than it had before. I needed to leave and leave now!

As usual, Sam was right on my trail, racing me to the car like he was the white dude in the movie the bodyguard. Just as I got to the door, I could see those same two sets of eyes but I still couldn't place the faces.   Though I am a vampire, I know there are things that can't   be explained about me and my parents would only tell me..

"Remember you are not the biggest fish in the pond..."

However true that may be, I *am* definitely

the most dangerous. I was also warned that true believers in GOD could always render me powerless. There was also the threat of male vampires. For some reason, they wanted to find the most powerful one and dominate her for all eternity. I am no one's slave!

Sam stayed with me and I enjoyed him all night long. We never came up for air and he no longer needed orders; he was more than willing. My appetite grew during the night so Sam left and came back with two new toys. Each one of them had their way with me. Sam was learning very well. Maybe a little too well? But, for now, I will continue to cum.

My body moved in such a way, I felt for a moment as if I was floating in mid air. It was total bliss. I could feel the blood of each man running through his veins. My lips were sucked on, my body was stroked, my nipples were licked like ice cream cones. Drippings of whip cream covered me as cream oozed down lips and fingertips. Our bonding made permanent that night as each one succumbed to my uncontrollable desire. I never wanted to leave this moment but I could still feel something deep within. Something that I could hear calling to me through my moans of pleasure and pain. The faster I fucked, the louder the voice got until pain was the only way to drown it out. I begged Sam to slap me.. Confused as he was he pulled back and slapped me with open palm!

"Hit me harder you bitch ass nigga!"

Each time I started to hear the voices, I begged to be hit. By the time the sun started to climb out of night, I was extremely beaten and at the hands of myself. Sam and I never spoke a word of it especially since we both knew that within hours I would look as if nothing had happened to me. That's another perk.

"So tell me of these voices that you keep hearing Helena?" He asked with extreme caution.

"I'm not sure what's going on but I need to figure this out. Maybe I just need to stay in for a few days and be alone..." I got no argument from him; he wanted me all to himself anyway.

*I think that's exactly what I need. Maybe I'm doing too much. I feel as if my blood is boiling and my heart is racing and the hairs on the back of neck are standing... I even felt like I was catching a cold which is something that I heard about years ago when my parents were alive. They would talk about how co-workers would be jealous of them because when germs or colds ran rampant, they would be immune to them. Sometimes I think my mother wished to be human but my father was very proud of who we are. Me, I couldn't careless but being this way made my life very comfortable. I didn't have to have a job being a vampire... my parents were able to capitalize on all sorts of stocks and bonds to make sure I never worked a day in my life. I did take jobs here and there... I mean it is 2014 and Philly night life is always jumping. Besides, I think my neighbors would really attempt to investigate if they never saw me leaving for work at night...*

# Ramone

I had been in for days and was feeling so much better. Maybe all I really needed was some rest but now I was thirsty. At this point, if I didn't hurry up and feed my desire, I would result to animals and that just ain't my style.

The night air felt so sexy tonight. My sheer skirt showed off my beautiful brown thighs as the light wind blew. I had purchased a pair of sexy black strapped heels with silver spikes and tossed on my waist short leather Donna Karen jacket. I wanted to break up some of this black so I had my silver clutch bag. Out for a night stroll in Ritten House Square, couples held hands and painters sat on benches honing their craft. Some of these artists, in my opinion, were brilliant! It's funny how I could enjoy life's little pleasures while loving the destruction that I created. It's A Vampire Thang You Wouldn't Understand.

There was a smell in the air just out of my reach but it was so strong and powerful I couldn't ignore it! I licked my lips just thinking of who could be that fucking inviting. I picked up my pace as to come face to face with the smell. For a moment the smell was so alluring that small beads of sweat started to form around my top lip. My hands began to shake and I was being control by a force beyond my comprehension. Every fiber in me raced towards the smell that now sat in the pit of my stomach and then it happened...The voices were back, only this time I could make out what they were saying. They turned into a him.

I saw him from a distance and I slowed my walk as to not look like I was rushing. He walked toward me talking on his cell phone. As we approached one another, he looked up from his conversation and said...

"Peace Queen how you doing?" I nearly fainted as he spoke from the overwhelming scent of him. Not in a foul nature, but of everything that was not me since...well I lived on the plantation. I froze and maybe he noticed that something was wrong so he asked me if I was OK?

"Maybe you should have a seat Queen you don't look too good."

"Why do you keep calling me Queen?" He laughed and I was caught up in him.

"Well, that's what I call black women because that's what you are, Beautiful Black Queens."

He looked at me and again asked if I was OK or if there was someone that he could call to come and get me. I told him no and he said he would stay for a few minutes just to make sure because it was night and his mother raised him that way. We talked for at least an hour and finally I asked him if I wanted to run into him again where would I find him. His answer was...The Clothes Pin at City Hall.

I watched his lips as he spoke every word but then it was as if I had to look away. I felt as if he could read my thoughts.   It was so powerful my body felt as if it were being pulled towards him though I made no movement.

"So can I ask you something?"

"Shoot." He seemed so relaxed and carefree.

"What's your name?"

"Oh, I'm sorry...my name is Ramone." I laughed.

"What's funny?"

"Nothing.. I just never met a black man with

such a well, you know."

"Well, now that I've shared my secret...why don't you tell me yours?"

"My name is Helena." That was all I was telling, though for some reason I wanted to tell him all.

"Well Ms. Helena, how possible would it be to get your math?" I guess by the expression on my face he could tell I had no idea what he was talking about.

"Your number." Now it was his turn to laugh.

"Oh, of course...I'm sorry my mind went someplace for a second."

"Are you sure you're alright walking alone. I could take a detour just to make sure you get to your front door." I was so very, very tempted. The scent was maddening.

"That would be nice but I have to be somewhere. Maybe we could do something tomorrow... that is... if you call me."

"I'm definitely going to call you. You take care of yourself out here."

Once he walked away, I sped up my walk

and walked smack dab into a fight! This can't be happening. As I watched for a moment, the couple exchanged curse words and fist, it enraged me to know that in a moments time he would overpower her and beat the shit out of her and then it happened. That blow to the face that always sent a woman to the floor incapable of getting up and continuing her fight!

"Bitch stay the fuck down this time! Get back up and not only will I beat that ass but I'll fuck around and kill you out here!"

As this poor girl lay halfway in the alley, face down crying, I couldn't help but take this opportunity to introduce myself.

"I don't know what she did but she must have messed with the wrong man. That's the problem with these young chicken heads they don't know how to treat a man."

He turned around quickly as if he still had some fight to finish. He took a look at me from head to toe and spoke.

"I'm not like that but this chick did some crazy shit to me but never mind that...what is a fine ass such as yourself doing walking the streets this time of night?"

My lie came so swiftly I believed it myself.

"My boyfriend just broke up with me and tossed me out of his car..." I let a coupe of blood tears drop but it was too dark and he was too fixated on my body to notice all but a sniffle.

"You need to let me walk you home just to make sure you're safe."

This bastard had no idea he was about to be my dinner.

"You would do that for me?" I sniffed just a tad louder.

"Hell yes, if I could get a hug or something... I mean, damn, your body is crazy! I can't stop looking at it. That nigga must have lost his mind to toss out a treasure."

"I love hugs but you know what I like even more than hugs...fuckin."

He stopped dead in his tracks with his mouth wide open as if he wanted to say something but didn't. Since he was speechless, I took the opportunity to lure him in.

"I always wanted to do it out in the open where people could see..." I gave him a look that told the whole story. He pulled me close, putting his fingers inside of me. I acted as if I was being touched for the first time. He moved my skirt out of the way and squeezed me between his fingers.

"You want this?"

"Yes." I was breathless for real.

"Tell me you want it."

"Fuck me baby. Make me squirt this juice all over you."

At that second, he lifted me up by my frame and sat me on his massive dick. It was hard, thick, long, and pulsating. My back was being scraped against the brick wall and it started to burn but nothing was taking me away from this feeling. He pulled me up and it was like a stopper letting out the water in a tub. Cum ran down my legs and all over him. The trash can would have to hold me up as he bent me over it and entered from behind. My pussy opened up to him like a blooming flower.

"Damn baby, where the fuck you come from?"

Each stroke came with more force until he pulled out and came all over my ass! My body was almost satisfied. He stood against the wall holding his manhood as I walked closer to him. This would be the first time I allowed anyone to see my fangs. He stood frozen as I sank my teeth into him! I was so hungry that I left just enough blood in him to still have a little color but his body shook with such force that he fell to the grow, which allowed my teeth to drag across his skin as if two razor blades had been used to kill him. I had not actually killed anyone in some time but he deserved it. I may be a vampire but I'm a woman as well...

For the past few weeks, Ramone and I have been talking on the phone about everything from religion to education and a lot about sex. I wanted him so badly. There was something so very different about him. He could hold my attention and even make me jealous when he mentioned other women. I have never felt insecure or intimidated until now. I wanted to make sure I kept our relationship completely based on phone conversations because being around him drove me past the point of controlling myself. He was smart, sexy, and interesting. He was able to make me laugh as well as make me sad. When he talked to me, all I could do most of the time was zone out. Not because he was uninteresting but because I felt some type of hypnotic spell being cast. Not much different from the one I cast over my spellbound victims.

Finally, during one of our conversations, he asked if he could come over. I didn't know what to say but "yes" came out so fast I didn't realize I was the one saying it.

"So what's a good time for you? How about around 12 noon?" Yeah...Right!

"How about after 8pm because I don't get off of work until 6pm and that will give me time to get a shower etc?" I had to make it convincing.

"That sounds fair."

"Good, I will see you at 8."

When I hung up the phone, I felt butterflies in my stomach and couldn't sit still. Imagine, a blood sucking vampiress with nervous butterflies. I cleaned my place, cooked something and put on something sexy. I wanted him to know from the door that I wanted him but I felt something else that I couldn't put my finger on. I told Sam to go away for a while and I would call him soon. He was such a puppy. Tonight I wanted no interference.

He walked in the door, his scent once again overpowering me. I tried to act natural but he noticed and laughed.

"What's so funny?" Nonchalant was really not working for me.

"Nothing Queen." There he goes with that queen stuff again.

"Wow you have a really nice place here. I love the decor....Mmm, smells good too. I see you can get busy in the kitchen."

"I do OK."

"So..." he settled down on the sofa to ask his questions; I was prepared, "... do you mind if I ask what you do for a living?"

My lies were coming with ease now.

"I'm a registered nurse."

"I figured   it had to be something like that because you seem like the caring for people type." Mmm...really. Was he talking about me?

We sat, had dinner, talked and laughed a

lot.    I put on some soft music and we danced. He was a very good dancer. It seemed as if he was too good to be true. After dinner, we stood on my balcony, overlooking downtown Philly.

Without warning, he turned to me, pulling me close. I could barley stand by this time. He was intoxicating and enchanting in every way possible. This mysterious Mr. had swept me off of my feet and I couldn't care less. He slowly pushed his tongue in my mouth and I tasted such sweetness. With each suck and slurp of my lips he pulled me in closer. My lips belonged to him. He told me he'd been looking for me all of his life and that destiny had forced this union. I am by now totally in his control.   He led me to my bed, laying me down so softly. He looked at me as if we had been in love for our entire lives. I couldn't believe what was happening. I had never felt like this before.

He stroked my hair with such gentleness, speaking to me in such a way it had me open to the possibility of change. *What is he doing to me*, I thought to myself. He began to softly kiss my shoulders, my nipples. He sucked on them first softly, then with a gentle force. He went down to my stomach and then between my legs.

"Mmmmm don't stop...Ooh baby please don't stop."

He looked up, demanding I tell him I'd been a bad girl and I want to be spanked. He wanted me to tell him that I sucked another man's dick and deserved to have my ass spanked. I said everything he wanted me to say and then some. He grew more excited each time I went into detail about being with another man. It turned me on too.

He made me say and do things I'd never done with anyone else and for the first time, I wanted someone to fuck me in the ass. I was nervous and scared but so more than willing to go there. He had the power to make me do whatever he wanted. His dick was so inviting and it curved up like a hook each time he pulled out. I never wanted him to pull out. I wanted it. He pulled me by my shoulders down to him, talking to me, telling me how he was about to push all the way in my ass.

"Suck my dick baby."

The way he said it had me instantly ready to cum. I got on my knees while he sat back on my lounge chair and glided my mouth up and down his dick. I kissed it so softly as to let him know I loved it. I slurped it, played with it; jerked it and pulled on it but not too hard. The saliva from my mouth was everywhere! I grew more and more excited from having his perfect proportions hitting the back of my throat that I unknowingly bit him! I couldn't stop myself! I kept sucking and pulling and growing more eager! I sucked his dick as if my life depended on it and he loved every bit of it. He pulled my head down on him even harder and when I finally came up blood and cum was everywhere!I thought for certain he wouldn't understand what had just happened but instead he kissed me so hard, we shared every bit of him. I couldn't explain this feeling but no human had ever made me feel this way.

My hands began to shake and my body grew stiff as I looked him in the eyes; a tear formed in the comer. I couldn't imagine what could possibly bring this man to tears..

After a moment, I realized my body was still stiff and as I grew colder, even my hands began to wrinkle as if I was rapidly growing older by the second. I looked down to see my heart being held in the palm of Ramone's hand. The light from it was slowly fading away as he began to change into the priest that had killed my parents. I had always said one day I would go back for him but had no idea he would come for me.

"As I said to you, I have been looking for you my entire life Helena." The thing I saw was the face of every victim unfortunate enough to cross my path.

He would crush my heart into fine grains of dust and watch my body fade away before he himself faded into the night...

# Penetrating Poetry

## My Body Addiction

My hands long to touch you
My lips long to kiss you
My thighs beg for your attention
My juice flows for you
My voice begs for your thrust
My hips feel your push
My eyes smile and dance seeing your
manhood
We speak in the language of lust
It drips from my lips
And you sip
Giving just the tip
I'm addicted to it

# Push Me

Push me past I love you

Show me the way

I have grown way too tired of leading

Let me follow you

But please don't sit and watch me crumble
only to shake your head with I told you so

Fast into the wind

Hold me to it

Push negative thoughts away

Push me to the bed

Push my arms over my head

Push my thighs to cradle you

Push me to burst

Push past the hurt

Push past yesterday and into tomorrow

## The Bus Ride

Too close we are...You breathe and I stop
Your toxins will not invade me unless I choose
Your voice thunderous...
You so undecided of which way to go
I will move mountains but I will not move you
Unfamiliar with your ways
You confuse me
Allow me to flee from you
You are a loud smelly bus passenger that I
came across today..

**Damn bus ride!**

# Slow Strippin

Seductively sucking on my bottom lip

Small beads of sweat begin to form over his left eyebrow

Sizing me up thinking on how he will lay me down

Hearts racing

I hear the sound of his emotions

They call to me and I attempt to fight

My body said yes long ago as pockets of explosives form between my legs

One touch and puddles will form in the middle of this room...

Damn Daddy

Your conversation sets me on a course of utopia

Caught in a delicious thought of us

My moisture begins to become noticeable

As my glistening grows

It becomes a shimmer in the darkness leading you

Guiding you

Fingers first

Now drenched with me...we share the all of everything

This feeling has me undressing with windows open

and stars twinkling off of bare nipples

Juice flows freely when he is close to me

Night winds slowly brush our beautiful brown skin as we prepare to taste and feast from the table of us

A nibble for him...

A bite for me...

Our bodies canvass

No area goes untouched

Strokes long and consistent

Painting a lustful portrait

# When You Are Gone

If you are not here with me
My fingers will have to do
No one gets me the way that you do
If you are too far from here
Your voice-mail will play in my ear
I will pinch my nipples and pretend that it is
you
I will tease my clit until you come and play
along too
Play your video
While I glide my dildo
Call your name as if you can hear me
If only you could see me Please daddy
come here Bring midnight near Bring
daylight too
Shit got me under a spell like voodoo

# He Can Get It

When I'm away from him I feel him in the
heartbeat of my inner
It reacts to his voice
I have no choice
Sucking his lips
Shit
Got it bad for that shit I can't have
Talk to me
I can't go a day without it
Give me that twist
Make me shiver Hard like liquor Fine like
wine Anytime
Got the shakes for you Whisper your name
My shit ain't the same This ain't no game
He can get it
Damn.. I'm twisted
Shouldn't have fucked with it

# Phone Sex

Don't make me
I can't
What if someone hears my moans? See me
biting my lip
Feels me gliding my fingers
Ears pressed hard to the phone
I taste your liquid love in m mind
You do it every time
Wanting you between my legs
Therefore, I almost forget that my phone is
not waterproof
Sips and grips Lips on tits Licks on stick
Then French kiss it
Shit

# I Want To

I want to I need to I have to
All types of ways Close ups and such Grip
the clutch Smack the butt Bust the nut
Dig all in these guts
Been so long
Doing me all types of wrong got me in my
goody bag day and night
Gels and creams
See what I mean?
Sex is he and he knows it
He has them captivated by his strong silence
and mystery
We sit and wait for him to speak and when
he does...my pussy heats up

# Take It from Here

Shouldn't have to explain myself to you but 1 will

Maybe I should not be so anxious to kiss you

Maybe I should slow down when it comes to crawling up between your thighs like jaws..

Why should I stop thinking of turning you over and licking you from head to toe

You just look so much like chocolate coated something to me and you know I love chocolate

I want to eat you up and swallow you and though I find myself putting myself out there for whatever..! just have gotten past the point of giving a damn

Don't   have time for what ifs

Should I? Maybe he?

I can't speak in any other language

I need to fuck you!

I have tasted lips like sweet wine

I have sucked on ripeness until juice danced from my lips to my chin

I have felt the heat from warm breath like a perfect mid summer breeze and I love it

I have read the words over and over until I had them memorized like a Patti Labelle song

How can any of this be wrong?

Caught up in some fantasy or nightmare

I am so clear on what I want and need and that is you

In every way imaginable in every way possible

I have watched the night sky in hopes that you may be looking out of your window at that very moment

I have closed my eyes and caught snow flakes on my tongue hoping that you would feel me and open yours also

Held so many conversations with you in your absence that your ears should be tired of listening    .

Said some sweet things

Maybe some not so sweet things

Gotten choked up

Said some stupid shit

I need your lips

Here

Now

All Over

# Tonight

Heels
Red Wine
Soft moist lips, both sets
My tongue pressed against yours Begging
for you to take it now! Do what you will!
But don't make me wait

# Remembering When

Sexed my mind long back when
A time not remembered by me
Just remember open mouth kisses to my
membrane
Pulsating dialect stimulating me for all time
Cells and veins activity at an all time high
My hand between my legs pressed up
against me so he can't hear me cum
Holding back beams of light
We speak of loving in bold bright regal colors
We flirt in exciting adjectives
We move like verbs at play all day We lay like
sand on black beaches When hurt we sting
like bees dying off
Continuously bumping our heads on the inside
of the jar lid
Your words slid past my lips and over my
gums
Down my throat and I choked on its thickness
but continued on and on..damn baby didn't
realize just how thick it was

# Watch the Curve

Gliding into paragraphs that turn into pages
Let our words take main stages
While we engage in
Word play..foreplay
Our story now a best seller on the list
And it ain't started with a poets kiss
And a word tryst
Debating long gone from my mind
Need a moment of your time
Though the curve in the words may be superb
Has nothing on what is yet to be heard
Switch positions
Your words be the key to my ignition
Scared of my own voice

Ssh setting the scene:
He comes into the room..all I see is his silhouette
And the silhouette is fine as hell!
The steam from the bathroom follows him out the door
Slits are my eyes from a long days work
I must be dreaming.. he moves slowly to the bed as my heart begins to beat a
little faster
The oils form his body makes me feel hazy and intoxicated all at once

## NIMA'S NIGHTS

The aroma fills my spirits and
commands me to quiver
Flexed
Sexed

# He Has Me

To this day I bid farewell
For the night calls me
It's where he dwells waiting for this day
walker
It is where our shadows meet and dance
until dawn
No one knows that we are there
His touch sends me past ecstasy
I crave him yet I pretend not to be bothered
His lips make me slip into another world
His voice puts me into a state of
unimaginable pleasure
Being with him sends me soaking
My heart fluttering
That look in my eyes he knows all too well
Telling me what I will and wont do..damn
baby
You just don't know
Feared that these feelings were long gone
and then.... Here you are

## Secrets

I really need to let you in on something
Since you seem to be oblivious to my ways
I can't imagine being in this room without
you
I have been opening my heart, legs, and my
words to you
Inviting you in is a constant reminder of
desire
Passion swims through each syllable
Tongue drips letters that spell out your name
Come bring me heaven Warm bodies like
thunder Bolts like lightening
Yes Yes baby! Show me the way

# Make

I want to make love to him on the pages of
my words
Missing him so makes me want to allow our
words to make lust
Make love Make music Make wet Make
sunsets
Make moonlight
Make us all over the book and not give a
damn who looks

# His Art Work

This blank sheet is her body untouched
unblemished under no pressure His smooth
tip and full body gathers close to her and
she can feel him...stroke
Now erect and excited he begins his pre
cum state
He looks over her entirely and draws near
Soft kisses at first with one or two
words...stroke
Seeing how willing she is... his flow
increases faster and smooth
Steady and pure
His explosion has created a serious
masterpiece and he has sealed it with a
kiss
Damn I love this shit!

# Orchestra

The man of my hearts song
That specific melody
High notes
Low tones Sex moans Spirits dance
Had all of me before time Gravity has that
hold... That pull
Scripture type Pre-ordained Then
re-arranged
Sometimes strange how we happened upon
One another
Love past the next planet

# Free

I need every drip of him
Tasting his sweat is one of my many desires
I want him to myself Exchanging sex
sounds Love noise
Matching each pump with my heart beat
Coughing because my throat is extra dry
from an open mouth that wont close
Confused
Lost turned out maybe? I need you baby!
That sofa is calling us
That floor seems inviting
That bed may get jealous but not for long
I need an (our song)
Promise me that
Let me lay you on your back
Kiss you into sleep
Then let it go deep
Toss all of your writings onto the floor
I don't   care anymore
Let's wet every one of them
Then to the back you play around the rim
Been said please
Been on my knees
This shit is deep for me
With you is where I want to be
I just need to be FREE
Made for you and whatever we decide to do
In our place at our appointed time

# NIMA'S NIGHTS

We make stars appear out of nowhere
We love from sunset to moon-glow
Parting only momentarily to gaze into one
another's eyes
Yesterday has been loved away Tomorrow is
having foreplay with today We stand dead
center of it all pushing love
Kissing love Exploring love Touching love
Loving love and all that it offers
I love love
And I love us

## So Much Better

The image of him in my mind
More powerful than the reality of someone
else
I speak to him as if some how sound wave
and vibrations will seek him out The mind
controls the body and he has controlled it
for some time. However, he does not have a
clue
Desires so strong
Though I smile when he approaches..
I look away in fear that he may know how
much I want him
My inner voice screams I love you
However, shouting is not appropriate
I want to wrap my arms around his neck
while standing on my tiptoes
Kiss his lips and touch his nose
Feel his skin
Smell him until his smell leaves with me
I just want him with me

# We Are Who We Are

I am a writer
I write
I am a lover..! love
He is a commander He commands me
He is a leader
He leads me into him
I come without thought
Without hesitation
I am overdosed on his medication
Swallowing every bit
Injecting that shit
Bit by bit
He slid up in it Got me on twist
Tripping for it
Sucking on my bottom lip
Introduced me to it against the wall
My mouth warm and inviting

Let us do it in continuous rotation
Lay next to you
Eyes never part until sleep comes
Come sleep but come slow Don't want to
rush rapture Passing pleasures in waves
Consistent of a tsunami
But only death to boundaries and limits
Spinning days into night and the curving of
my spine mandatory
Past sex past lust past love making

Entered into unknown long ago Attempting to smile in the face of fear While you enter my temple

Shakes and moans take shape and become like boogie men coming from my closet

You pretending to calm my emotions while your ego sips more of me

My darkness speaks in hush tones yet you still hear the whispers coming from between my legs

Your heart beat becomes our rhythm

It is good

Pride is off limits

Like the beat of a Congo it is spiritual Knees bend at command then toes curl Your woman I am

# I asked

Is it too much to ask? White wine
Your favorite poem
Low light
In bed
Me on your chest listening to you read after
we mix it up
Sweat and us!

All I asked for was for you to leave..
Your clothes at the front door
Allow me to take away the stress of your
day
Allow me to play
In your arms, fingers down your chest
Promise to do my best
Whisper stories untold Unleash your soul
Penetration upon relaxation Upon further
investigation
Leading to continuous masturbation

# Overnight Open Mic

Queen steps in the room
He wants her to sing into the mic
Even if she doesn't   spit
Just wants her to blow on it a little bit Ass as
brilliant as the perfect moon Refuse to come
to quick
Sometimes soft with it
Other times hard hit that shit
He been waiting for her to spit
Just may have that flow to wet his girl a
little bit
Don't trip
Let her drip
Into something hot
Give me all you got
Brown skin like dirt
Bet you want to get under the skirt
Don't get hurt
Drama with my king it ain't worth
Body straight from the Motherland
Meaning that shit wide open til some need
stitches

# How should I put this?

Everyday I can hear myself telling you I
love you
Everyday I can feel myself being in love
Am I selfish to want this feeling as much as
possible?
Does it make me self-centered to want all of
your attention? Surround myself with all of
you
Do the things that gods of love would do
Travel through the night's sky just to find
the brightest star and place it in your hand?
I want to feel your skin until it is no longer
your skin but our skin
Kiss you until forever
Look into your eyes and become focused on
all possibilities
We have long passed the point of physical
lovemaking
It is a spiritual and emotional reckoning
between the two of us.

# Secrets on Paper

Secret notes
We hold silent
Inspired by one another's pen
Let us begin
To ink our destination without hesitation
Images that only we see
This thing pre-ordained will not let us be
Accepting you in before your ink dries Eyes
roll back
My pen to the sky
We fly
Because it's where we have landed
This ink.. this us.. being apart..
I just can't stand it
Accidentally words dropped from my lips
Before I could get a grip
I slipped and fell hard into his shit

# Re-charge

Thought this feeling was long gone Put
these feelings on the back burner Long
forgot them
Fine with them in the past
You startled my soul in such a way My
emotions took a journey into you I don't
want to return
Came into this place and gathered my hearts
song
Sang into it
I love duets

# Talent

Talent can be found if you look hard enough
within
But can you really look around?
Talent can't be found as in a lost and found
Talent can't be bought It comes from within
Beyond a thought
We can sit here and think...we don't have it
When we really do have it
You just have to bring it out!
Without a doubt you can bring your inner
talent out!

Written By..Lexis M. Harris

# He Writes

When he writes I get Goosebumps
When he spills his ink I tremble
When his pen is erect, I am so focused on it
Eyes closed
Afraid to breathe
For I may awaken from this dream
More like a fantasy Wishing it was reality In
and out of emotions Feeling bipolar
His meticulous use of words penetrate me
and I beg for more
His metaphors tease my breast and now they
stand waiting for him
Panties soaked from his delivery
My inner no longer my own at least until he
finishes his post
Eyes peering through me
I have loved him most likely in a far away
land long before this world existed
I love him far beyond what's    between his
legs...although like his words that too holds
power and I've kissed it
I want to shower him with all of me
Whatever he wants me to be
As long as we are a we..See?
All it took was that split second
That one moment in time that we wish, we
could get back
That rewind

That do over
Words exchanged in fits of rage Intended
target straight ahead 20 paces Red dots pin
point kill shots
We take aim and let hate fly
Fly through the air Pressed up against skin
Attempting penetration Clenched teeth
speak anger Unseen until now
Oppressed and hidden by time Time, which
took hidden tolls We paid unknowingly

# Don't turn Away

Forgot my scriptures still
I see the big picture
Bible in my left hand Koran in my right
Calling Allah..Yahweh..Jehovah at night
Making sure to cover everything just to get
it right

Jesus hangs around my neck
But I'm still caught up in bustin those
checks

I got a fuckin problem
I'm trying to solve em

Never pulled da burner on a cat dat didn't
deserve it
Still shed tears still felt it

Sin got me getting wetter
My Moorish family taught me better

On my knees praying the spirit moves me
But I got caught up in puffin and watching
gangsta movies

Raised by street life Educated maniac
Plotting til its ova Help me JEHOVAH!

## NIMA'S NIGHTS

So I'm a sinner
So I don't deserve to be saved
Yet they still don't walk on the road of
righteous that you paved
Bat signal in the air
I refuse to believe that you don't    care
Pages of my bible show me
Rape, robbery betrayal, murder

Took his son to the bushes on a bed of sticks
put the knife to his neck
And they wonder why I'm a wreck

The other created a Ark preparing for the
flood My streets flooded with blood and I
can't swim Making love to a bottle of Gin
I'm trying to find my way back to you
Father through him.
Your son
Journey just begun

# Traumatized

Because he touched her way too soon
Because he learned to use a gun before a
fork or spoon
Because she watched, her mother beat
continuously
Because being poor was the thing to be
Because there were two at the top and two
at the bottom
Because if one came home with chicken pox
They all got em
Because shooting dice was a come up on
rent day
When he walked out the door When you
begged him to stay Because bills wont wait
You go out with a few more dates

When dreams take a back seat because you
need that money
When you deliver a package
But you feel somewhat funny
When the men she loves never add up
Because she loved her daddy so much
Maybe because she gave her all to someone
that didn't give it back

Maybe because she was beat so much that
She thought love was blue and black
So often thinks of the one that got away

Never understood he was not there to stay
Have yet to meet her match though he has
caught her eye
Can she really be happy from being
traumatized

# What Is This

We make nice conversation
Share smiles and stories of yesterday Hands
shake pass friendly gesture His smell sends
me right back
The way he positions his feet
A serious stride
Sometimes I wonder if his feet touch the
ground
I wonder if his arms are still strong
The pull That lure That force Damn
Laughter fills the air around us
Then an awkward silence
Too quiet to ignore
We walkaway

# Dreams May Come True

Only in my dreams we love, laugh, play,
live, kiss
Touch me all day
Conversations    all day
Poetry or spoken word this is what we do
Just us two
I chase him but only in my dreams
We smile
He holds me
Tells me he loves me
Make music to my lips

# Sunrise

I promise you I saw a sun Just peeking over
the hills Just before 6:45am
I thought of it in my dreams the night before
and it sang to me
It made such a sweet sound
It whispered through the clouds
Hushed the birds
In addition, began to melt away the frozen
cage
I thought I saw a sunrise

Sometimes I need to sit in a dark room
Sweep out cobwebs with this mental broom
Platting to seal your doom
Thinking it may be too soon Naw you
deserve two guns Two cannons
North bitches do damage
You can't stand it
Cause now I'm rammin
She so sweet She so nice Chocolate pudding
Just enough spice
We never seen that side of her

Where dat come from
Came from what you lames done done
Took what I said and spun Bring it to my
face I dare you Oh now you don't want to
Mmm..I calls that a bitch move

Some back in the day crush groove
Never hype
I stay smooth
Check my smile seems a little off
What's behind the eyes? Could it be a
disguise?
Some say oh no queen never refer to
yourself as a bitch
Drastic times drastic measures
Watch the moves of a few
So sometimes, it is the fuck whatever
My queen never takes a back seat to
anything But getting in those ditches ain't
about a thing If I have to ask my king to
hold my crown
So I can step down to meet a bitch on her
level
Then we all must dance with the devil
But while I'm dancing the two step
I got gods light held to my chest
I may act crazy but I know what is best
You talks lots of shit about me
But stay asking how I be?
That fake-ism
You live for that lame-ism
Cartoons are what you lames are to me
That's why I'm changing the station B.

# Bloody Apple Tree

Hung that man down by the apple tree
I know because they came for me
Saw we was in love!
He read to me love letters he had written!
Beat that man for knowing those words!
Wanted to know who taught him to read! He
never told them that someone was me
I learned it from my father who came on a
slave ship... who was a doctor before the
trip
I cried and begged them to spare his life
They hung that man from the apple tree
because of me

## Excuses Part 1

Twisted Dreams Fuckin screams Track
marks Cold hearts
Bullet to the brain Kicked in the door frame
Soul running down the drain Bitch ass
Gun blast
Committed to this way of life
Demonic life style
Bugged off that laced chronic Sippin that
hypnotic Relationship toxic
Spit poison
Just to kill the noise and ... Eyes blood shot
red
Giving me head
But my senses dead Stalking dark streets
Trying to creep
Ain't shit sweet

# Visions

Cried in my sleep as I saw visions of black
faces being sold off as cattle
Tears I am unable to hold back as husbands
tom away from wives
Mothers ripped away from their own
children only to be replaced by the white
mans babies
Giving life forces to that which has been
birthed by our oppressors
Cook, clean farm and teach their young how
to pray.
Praying you have enough to give to your
own
Beaten and rapped until near death
But death sometimes sweet death will have
to come knocking another time for now it is
my own blood that calls to me.
My own blood that needs to be fed and
cleaned You go away death.
I am caring for my own skin My kin

# Jesus Save Me?

The devils riding next to me
So to prove I've been going to church I got
Jesus in my selfie
Some one help me! Must I help myself?
Don't want your fools gold because this
earth don't hold my wealth
Got me twisted off that religion you gave
me

Dysfunctional so my grandparents prayed
for me
Said they saved me
Sin made me
Pulled me out this pit
Done with this shit
Looking in the rear view at my past life
Knowing damn well that shit wasn't right
They say two wrongs don't make a right
I was knee deep at the time and it felt just
right

Walking down the aisle begging preacher
man to lay hands on me
Don't turn me away
This where the sinners be
Let me know you care for me
Look...I'm doing the dance singing the
songs

Putting money in the plate what else am I
doing wrong?
Smoked filled rooms dimly lit

Cleared her throat before she gave us a little
bit
Had us all back then snapping our fingers
and wearing funny hats
Calling one another -Daddy 0 and Hip Cats
Chasing long black pencil skirts with tight
stripped black and white shirts holding big
tits

Sitting in cramped spots unplugged jukebox
Smoked rings circle my head as I await for
The poetic bombshell to speak
She opens her mouth and I was hooked
Tapping my vein searching for the right spot
to inject some more of her

She is a Jezebel when she speaks
We hang on every word
Each syllable
Trapped in her eyes while she delivers
I burn the tips of my fingers forgetting to
pluck ashes
She finishes with a ..that's right jack and can
you dig that

Now poetry and spoken word is a battlefield
covered with dope Emcees and newbies

Everyone with his or her chest out with cocky arrogance
Where is the romance?
It walked away with a long black pencil skirts and a funny hat
With men and women calling one another daddy 0 and hip Cat

# Why Write?

I must write
I have to write
My pen pushes forward
It guides me though I am not clear on much
It writes until there is no more ink
It bleeds needing a transfusion
0 negative to be exact
Positive that my pen will live on long after I
am gone

Every dream seems a little more realistic
Every daydream seems more like a reality
Every whisper seems so clear
My vision is no longer clouded
My resistance is low and your invasion is
accepted
Virus filters through my system
The matrix has been compromised
My walls of defense begin to crumble into
piles of rubble then into ashes

# In The Sky

Let us go away on your spaceship
Your lights I saw, as I stood naked in the
middle of the fields
The greens, reds, silvers, golds made me
breathless
Your light I love Glowing Shimmering
Warming my soul
Unaware of what is in store I am amazed
and afraid
Yet I walk towards the open door hoping for
eternity

# Dream Ships

Gazing catching figures Figures of who I use
to be Lost somewhere in you Forgot what
lives in me Making you all
Days and nights lost on dream ships that go
nowhere
Pulling in Port after Port Unknown destination
Smells through out the air
Waters seem unsteady and my focus is lost
Lighthouses are dim

Hearts dark just like that Sun stopped
shining Such as life
Happens now again
Some lose love like friends Pick that shit up
keep stepping Grounds seem a little shaky
Falling may be strong possibility Getting up
is harder but do so
Crawling may have to start you off
Crawl to walk
Walk to run
Run towards the sun
Leave gloom in the past
Gloom lurks waiting for opportunity to play
It never last
However, it remains hidden in the corners of
our minds and heart

# Sexy Suggestions

*You will not find happiness between the legs but you will find satisfaction...*

*Taste her daily and problems will be at a minimum...*

*Love is a beautiful thing...just do not forget to fuck!*

*Be A Gentleman But Fuck Her Like A Mad Man!*

*Lick my lips and I will lick you in return.. Gladly...*

*Expose your heart to your lover then expose your love all night long. You will not be sorry.*

# After Word

*Thank you so very much for taking the time to read my latest project. I appreciate all of the love, support, and criticism that you all have shown me during this time. I hope that after reading this you were left satisfied on some level. It is my goal to create some type of dialogue, infect your senses, and toss emotion and most importantly to leave you wanting more of me. As time goes on I will continue to grow and I hope that you will stay on for the ride. I promise it wont hurt unless you want it to..*

## Love & Lips...
## Nima

# Fighting

I hear the sounds of black faces against
the wind of despair
Fighting for change
Fighting for the right to be human
The winds of oppression is scattered
among their bones and they grow tired
Tired from pain and struggle
Tired from just getting by
My strength is in my color...it is in my
blood
Thousands of years, I went into
myself to find warriors...
Kings, Queens, Rulers, Leaders,
all so you can attempt to diminish
or abolish what we have done
The ignorance of some who allow and
believe in your trickery
You fool some but not enough into
forgetting their worth
I knew and I know...

*Nima*

# About the Author

*Nima*...

Born and raised in Philadelphia PA, has enjoyed reading and writing poetry and short stories since early childhood. She would learn to use her imagination and creativity to escape or break from the world around her.

Over time, she would learn to pull words and emotion from the same world she tried to escape. Through tragedy, pain, love, life, and lessons, she continues to write until she spills all of her ink or until she has nothing more to say.

Nima published her first work of art. *POEMS, QUOTES AND THOGHTS PROVOKED* in late 2014 with much success. In early Spring 2015, her creative spirit unleashed in a paint brush and she is now producing some awesome Impressionist's paintings. *Nima's Nights* is her second offering to the literary world.

With the love and support of her family, she will continue to grow and give all something to talk about. So, stay on the look out for Nima...